Deg

New *X Rated* titles from *X Libris*:

Game of Masks	Roxanne Morgan
Acting It Out	Vanessa Davies
Private Act	Zara Devereux
Who Dares Sins	Roxanne Morgan
The Dominatrix	Emma Allan
House of Decadence	Lucia Cubelli
Sinner Takes All	Roxanne Morgan
Haven of Obedience	Marina Anderson
Secret Fantasy	Vanessa Davies

The *X Libris* series:

Arousing Anna	Nina Sheridan
The Women's Club	Vanessa Davies
Velvet Touch	Zara Devereux
The Gambler	Tallulah Sharpe
Forbidden Desires	Marina Anderson
Letting Go	Cathy Hunter
Two Women	Emma Allan
Pleasure Bound	Susan Swann
Silken Bonds	Zara Devereux
Rough Trade	Emma Allan
Cirque Erotique	Mikki Leone
Lessons in Lust	Emma Allan
Lottery Lovers	Vanessa Davies
Overexposed	Ginnie Bond
G-Strings	Stephanie Ash
Black Stockings	Emma Allan
Perfect Partners	Natalie Blake
Legacy of Desire	Marina Anderson
Searching for Sex	Emma Allan
Private Parties	Stephanie Ash
Sin and Seduction	Emma Allan
Island of Desire	Zara Devereux
Hotel of Love	Dorothy Starr

Degrees of Desire

Roxanne Morgan

An *X Libris* Book

First published in Great Britain in 2001
by X Libris

Copyright © Roxanne Morgan, 2001

The moral right of the author has been asserted.

*All characters in this publication are
fictitious and any resemblance to real
persons, living or dead, is purely coincidental.*

All rights reserved.
No part of this publication may be reproduced,
stored in a retrieval system, or transmitted, in
any form or by any means, without the prior
permission in writing of the publisher, nor be
otherwise circulated in any form of binding or
cover other than that in which it is published
and without a similar condition including this condition
being imposed on the subsequent purchaser.

A CIP catalogue record for this book
is available from the British Library.

ISBN 0 7515 3087 5

Typeset by
Derek Doyle & Associates, Liverpool
Printed and bound in Great Britain by
Clays Ltd, St Ives plc

X Libris
A Division of
Little, Brown and Company (UK)
Brettenham House
Lancaster Place
London WC2E 7EN

www.littlebrown.co.uk

Title conceived by
rhughes – thanks, Ray!

Chapter One

'I'VE GIVEN UP SEX!' Alix Neville announced.

Lewis, sitting in the next workstation bay, looked across at her and goggled. 'What, for *good*?'

Alix sighed. She sucked at the tip of her long silver-blonde hair, holding the strand in her fingers. Rather than look at Lewis's kind expression, she gazed out of the office window at February rain.

'I'm not exactly doing too well lately, am I?' she said, attempting to sound wry but hearing plain hurt in her own voice. 'This last year, there's been Sam . . . and Ben . . . and Adrian . . . – respectively, two hours, two months, and two minutes! I think . . . I think I'm burned out. I'm just past it, Lew!'

The large black-haired man in the next workstation coughed unexpectedly and set his coffee cup down unsteadily by his keyboard. 'At twenty-nine? What does that make *me*?'

'Confident.' Alix swivelled idly in her chair, and watched raindrops slide down the glass of the office tower's window. Winter covered London in a freezing grey drizzle. Her skin shivered, a little, at the contrast between the chill outside and this heated office.

'It makes you confident,' she repeated. 'Men only get distinguished as they get older—'

'*Thank* you!'

'—and women still go for older men . . .'

Lewis's eyes crinkled as he looked across at her. 'Is this a proposition?'

She surveyed him, momentarily – Lewis Kumar, mid-thirties, dark; big, broad shoulders under his suit jacket: his arms would be strong, warm around her . . . In his embrace, she would feel small, fragile, subject to the glowing heat at her groin.

A sudden blast of wind slathered rain against the window beside her, the noise dimly penetrating even the glazing. Alix blinked. She smiled, and shook her head.

'Lew, you don't need to give me a charity fuck. And besides,' she added quickly, 'your girlfriend wouldn't exactly like it, would she?'

'I don't know: she can be quite adventurous . . .'

'*Lew*is!'

The big man smiled. 'You're just feeling down, sweetheart.'

'No. And I *am* giving up sex,' Alix said.

'I didn't know Ben and the others had had such a bad effect on you.' Lewis stood up and walked the couple of paces necessary to cross between their workstations. He put his hands on her shoulders.

She felt the warmth of his palms through the crimson silk of her shirt. Heavy, warm, dry . . . the scent of his cologne filled her nostrils. She found herself wondering, for a moment, what it would be like to be smelling it in a large bed, on clean sheets, among tumbled white pillows . . .

'You really are an attractive woman, you know.' His grip loosened, and he began circling movements with his thumbs, pressing them lightly into her shoulders below her neck. 'You shouldn't let a couple of bad experiences with a few men shatter your confidence...'

' "A couple"?' A squirt of panic chilled her stomach. All her shoulder muscles tensed, rock-hard. She realised she was waiting for Ben's voice: *You don't really think I'd want to live with you?* And Sam: *You're just some skinny little cow who thinks a blowjob is the height of erotic experience.* Then Adrian, supposed to be a care-free one-night stand...

'You know what?' she burst out, explosively. 'Adrian – he said I was a *bad lay*! He said fucking a mattress would be more exciting—!'

'Oh, *Alix*—'

'After all the things I've done, the last few years!'

'Alix.' He waited until he had her attention. 'When did *you* last enjoy a good lay?'

She felt her back stiffen. Thinking, she said at last, miserably, 'I don't know. Not recently. Maybe not for a long time... You know, Lew, three or four years ago, I would have had you right here across this desk—'

Glancing up, she saw him blink, startled.

'—never mind who might be looking – I was pretty wild then.[1] But now, I'm just... embarrassed. I can't do this. I can't even *want* to do this!'

Lewis lifted his hands away. Her shoulders were cold, missing his warm flesh. She heard his slightly ragged breathing calm down.

'Not your fault, Alix. They've really screwed you up, haven't they? The shits... But if you're not careful...' His dark brown voice took on a wry tone. 'If you go on like this, your virginity is going to grow back...'

---

[1] *Sinner Takes All*, Roxanne Morgan.

She almost laughed, but found herself too upset and confused. 'I like you, Lew, but—'

'Worst word in the English language, "but",' Lewis said. There was rueful humour in his expression. He turned towards his desk. 'Better get back to my firewall, I guess . . . I'm here if you ever want to talk. Or if you want a no-strings night.'

'You know, I never worked out how a straight guy like you got to be so—' *Sensitive,* Alix stopped herself saying. *Now there's a way to offend him* and *my gay friends!* She gave him a shaky little grin that soon faded into a grimace. 'Thanks . . .'

The monitor screen in front of her blurred, briefly, as she turned back to it, the lines of code running together. Her eyes stung. She felt an urge to lift her fists and bang them down on the keyboard – *Damn CompuForce, damn computer security programs, and damn me for giving up consultancy and taking a full-time job! But Ben approved of careful financial security . . . and now I guess I've got used to it.*

Lewis's scent of cologne and male sweat still lingered in the air. She pushed her mass of silver hair back off her face, feeling her cheeks warm against her palms. She felt unusually conscious of her body under her silk shirt and long skirt, her thighs flushing, her groin warm . . .

'No,' she said under her breath. 'What's the point? I'll only get told I'm a lousy lay again – and it'll be *worse,* coming from a friend.'

'We want you to retrain,' Dominic Harwood, the Human Resources Manager, said. 'This is a forward-looking company: I think you'll find it pays to keep up your place on the career ladder, Ms Neville.'

His smug voice grated. Alix thought, *If this was a*

consultancy, I'd tell you right *where to stick your personnel folder.*

Over Harwood's shoulder, the wide-screen office window looked out over the same view of London – with February's bitter cold replaced now by April's uncertain warmth, grey overcast skies by blue. The bright view failed to lift Alix's spirits. She had come into work this spring morning in her ratty old winter coat, and she'd been too hot in the Underground and too cold on the walk along the City's howling windtunnel streets. A feeling of physical unease suffused her body.

'What sort of retraining?' she asked, suddenly aware that he had been waiting for her to speak.

'We've signed you up for a computer MA at London University,' Dominic Harwood said, smiling. 'All the very latest developments in encryption, viruses, trojans . . . CompuForce needs someone at the cutting edge of that field of knowledge. Now,' he flicked over a page in the folder, 'we were going to release you part-time, next September, but fortunately we've found a place on an accelerated-degree-course module – if you start in two weeks at the beginning of the May term, you should be done by July at the latest. Of course, we wouldn't put you in unless we were confident you could handle it.'

Oh, great! And three months out of the office, Alix thought. *This smells like office politics to me. Who'll be sitting at my desk when I get back?*

'Do I care?' she mumbled, under her breath; and at his enquiring look, said aloud, 'Sure. I'll do it. Why not?'

A physical ache woke her. Almost unwillingly, her hand slid over her silky-smooth stomach, between her thighs: her middle finger seeking out the swollen lump of her clit. She lay dazed among sweat-sodden sheets, grabbing for the remnants of her dream as it sank out of her memory.

What was that? A man – but was it Adrian, or – and it looked like Sam, but different—

Her pelvis tilted, body seeking to eradicate the unsatisfied ache in her groin. Her finger slid in the juices of her cleft: hot, swollen flesh throbbing with the urge to climax.

No, but he was there: Ben—!

A flash of the dream came back to her. With it came the precise tone of Ben's voice. *'You don't like "string of pearls"? But then, you're not exactly feminine, are you?'*

Her body stopped, chilled. She worked her finger in her cleft, bruising her flesh, straining for the arousal of a moment before – gone, now. Her body as cold and unerotic as a fish on a slab.

'Oh, shit!' she moaned, and rolled over, dragging the duvet tight around herself. She shut her eyes against the yellow sun, and the cream walls, and the shadows of the wooden Venetian blinds on the floorboards. 'Shit, shit, *shit!*'

Two fingers, this time: she scrubbed at her clit with painful urgency, as if she could chase arousal and force a climax. Flesh remained inert, and she winced, the friction painful; and took her hand away, curled up, and pulled the pillow over her head.

This was my last weekend before the bloody university course; I was going to enjoy it . . .

Now I can't even come.

After a while, feeling her skin clammy and uncomfortable against the duvet cover, she got up. Hauling on T-shirt and jogging pants, she began to sort through her wardrobe for something that might be suitable for wearing on a mixed-age university computer course.

Preferably something old and comfortable . . .

'Oh, now, come on!' she addressed herself in the full-length mirror. 'Celibate, yes, but that doesn't mean you have to dress like a hag!'

The woman in the mirror looked back at her. A little over five feet seven inches tall, with a body neat from working out at the gym. Silver-blonde hair caught back in a French braid, now undoing itself, loose tangles sliding down over her shoulders . . . Her small, rounded breasts pushed against the old faded blue T-shirt. Where her black jogging pants slid down a little over her small hips, her flat stomach was visible, and her navel, where she had worn a piercing until – after Adrian's abrupt departure – it had made her feel like a schoolgirl straining after sophistication, and she had taken it out.

There's nothing wrong with how I *look*, she admitted to herself. It's just . . . me that's wrong, isn't it?

She slid her fingertips across her skin, between T-shirt and waistband. A shiver went through her. Where her bare feet touched the floorboards, she felt them cold, instead of sun-warmed.

I don't mean I won't ever be ready for another relationship – some time in the future. Maybe. If anyone ever wants me again, without getting bored after a few nights . . .

Alix set about digging out a reasonably plain T-shirt and a well-cut pair of black jeans.

University. Yoof culture. Eighteen- and nineteen-year-old students with wild sex lives, not twenty-nine-year-old women who're past it . . . Tutors who probably know less about computer security than *I* do. Oh, *won*derful . . .

'This,' she said aloud, 'is *all* I need.'

Two days later, she saw Fern Barrie for the first time.

Chapter Two

LONDON UNIVERSITY'S PARDOE COLLEGE lay south of the river. A blue morning sky gleamed. Alix drove through the green expanse of Blackheath, sparing a hand to push the button and lower the window of her new silver Audi. The scent of spring blew in, along with the tang of exhaust, and the chill of a breeze not yet quite used to being May.

Alix shook her loose hair back, revelling in the slipstream. Tendrils of hair caressed and tickled her bare shoulders. She swung the Audi round to park it in the college grounds: a square of tarmac surrounded by old, high-walled buildings. Crowds of students wandered past. Some were parking bikes; a surprising number had old bangers. Alix gave a small internal smile: *better to be a well-paid woman with a career than a debt-laden student . . . even if they are all eighteen and nineteen . . .*

Half an hour later, official paperwork done and lectures not due for another hour, she sat herself down in the self-service canteen. A rather watery cup of cappuccino steamed on the table in front of her, vapour rising silvery into the air. No doubt it smelled more delicious than it would taste, she thought.

As she took her cellphone out of her bag and flipped

down the menu to check unanswered e-mails, a laugh rang out from a table closer to the window. She glanced in the direction of the noise.

Large picture windows overlooked the courtyard below. A young man sat at one of the window tables with his back to the room. Facing him, a tiny brown-haired girl put her hand up over a wide smile and gave another smothered giggle.

She wouldn't be more than five feet tall, Alix saw. Her tousled brunette hair was cut off level with her ear lobes, and stood up in soft spikes. A leather biker jacket hung over the back of her chair. A white vest-type T-shirt, clip-fitting, strained over her small, adolescent breasts. Alix couldn't see below the table to see what else she might be wearing.

As the girl lowered her hand, and reached across the table towards the man – her boyfriend? – Alix glimpsed the silver glint of a piercing in her lower lip. A sudden flicker of interest surprised her.

With a wicked grin, the girl held her boyfriend's hand, dipped his finger down into the cream éclair on her plate, and lifted his hand to her mouth.

Her eyes were set widely spaced under arched, light brown brows. Alix couldn't see their colour from this distance. A few dots of freckles marked her cheek-bones. As she smiled, she showed white teeth – and, leaning forward, she nipped the man's cream-covered finger between them.

Alix craned forward herself, hoping to be unobtrusive, trying to catch a glimpse of the male student's face. She could see nothing of him except his dark curly hair and rugby player's shirt – on a rugby player's body, by the look of it: stocky and strong. A little short, but maybe not done with growing yet, and muscular . . . She wanted to see if his face was colouring with embarrassment, or if he had the broad grin of a man being abruptly and publicly turned on.

With a sudden shock that she felt as a jolt of adrenalin, the girl caught her eye.

Still holding the young man's finger between her teeth, she smiled at Alix. Then she closed her lips over the stiff, cream-covered flesh. Gripping his wrist between her two hands, she slid his wet finger in and out of her mouth: slowly at first. Fast. Faster . . .

Without conscious thought, Alix found her hand straying under the canteen table to her groin. Her clothes suddenly felt tight. She pressed a finger against the seam of her jeans, pushing it into her crotch, shifting her buttocks on the wooden seat. Her thighs tensed, flushing and heating.

Two tables away, the brown-haired girl looked past her boyfriend's shoulder at Alix, and slid the bare, glistening finger in and out of her mouth, lips pursed tightly around it.

The sun streamed in at the window. Chairs scraped on the tiled floor. A quick glance around – Alix saw no one nearby.

Still holding the cellphone in her left hand, she moved her right hand under the table to covertly undo the buttons of her black jeans. She slid her fingers inside, into hot, moist cloth. The fabric of her silk knickers was damp to her touch. She slid the pads of her fingers under the crotch of her knickers, pushing into the slick wetness there, stroking her clit with her stiff middle finger.

The brown-haired girl shifted her grip on the other student's wrist, dipping his finger down again to her plate, and lifting it dripping with cream. She smiled: a gamin grin. Slowly, she extended her tongue and licked the length of his middle finger, chasing a dribble of cream down into his palm, and over his wrist. A smear of cream shone on her chin.

Lifting her head again, she began at his thumb: pale pink tongue licking at the thick nail and wide knuckle. Licking him clean. And putting her lips around each fingertip in turn, sucking them into her mouth . . .

Alix felt the straps of her bra dig into her shoulders as her whole body tensed. Her breasts swelled, under her T-shirt; nipples throbbing and tender. Convulsively, she rubbed between her legs at her clit, finger slick with her own juices, skin flushing with the heat of her arousal.

In front of her, the man's chair scraped back as he stood up.

Before Alix could react, the girl stood up too – neither of them more than nineteen, by the look of it – and moved around the table to stand next to him. She reached her arms up and put them around his neck. The sunlight from the window illuminated her bare skin. She wore the skimpiest, tightest pair of shorts, and her tanned legs stretched their muscles to the full extent, standing on tiptoe in old faded trainers as she pressed herself to the length of his body, moulding herself to him, and Alix could almost feel against her own crotch the swelling bulge of his hard-on—

Because he must be turned on, he isn't human if he isn't!

Hell, I haven't had that much experience of women, and *I*'m turned on . . .

The silvery clatter of cutlery in the kitchen brought her back to herself. She realised she was staring at the two young students, jammed together in an embrace, him bending his head to lick at the piercing in her lip, slide his tongue down her chin to her throat as her head went back . . .

What am I doing?

Alix quickly, and with as little sign of it as possible, slid her hand out of her crotch and buttoned her jeans. She smelled the warm, bedroom scent of arousal on herself. She glanced around hastily. No one was staring at her. Of the half-dozen students left in the canteen, two were engaged in intense conversation, and the other four were transfixed by watching the brown-haired girl and her boyfriend.

Alix squirmed in her seat. The hard wood pressed the seam of her jeans against her clit. It was all she could do not to rock against it until she reached release – *but I'm in public, for God's sake, and I'm not nineteen*!

She lowered her gaze to her cellphone, eyes down. Even so, she was aware when they passed her, arms wound around each other's bodies, barely able to move for being pressed so close together. She didn't look up to catch the girl's eye, or stare at the man's bulging crotch. The unsatisfied ache in her cunt demanded, with a raw hunger, that she should. She forced herself to ignore it.

No. What's the point? If I'm a bore to men my age, that boy – and that girl – would just *laugh* at me . . .

At the induction lecture an hour later, a slender brown-haired girl in a biker jacket dropped on to the fold-down seat next to her. Resting her chin on her fingers, and her elbows on the long curving desktop that stretched away around the amphitheatre, she gazed across the hall full of chattering students for a minute, and then looked back at Alix.

'Fern,' she said, and gave a quick grin: 'It's my name, not a pot plant. Fern Barrie. Hi! Hey, isn't it great here?'

The young woman looked around with undisguised delight.

'And, hey,' Fern Barrie added, her gaze falling on a

cluster of male and female students towards the back of the hall, 'will you look at all the talent that's here this year!'

Towards the end of the first week, after several brief friendly conversations in passing, Alix found Fern Barrie falling into step with her again as she walked out of the library and made her way down the echoing stairwell to the college's entrance hall.

'Hi, again!' Fern grinned.

'Hi,' Alix said, charmed despite herself by the young woman's open friendliness. She made an effort to throw off her own depression. 'You off somewhere interesting for the weekend?'

'Nah. Can't afford it. Just going back to Yannis Road.' She held her black biker jacket slung carelessly over one shoulder, and the ring piercing her lip shone silver as they walked out of the building and down the steps together. She turned towards the row of parked bikes, then glanced back over her shoulder at Alix.

'Adam fancies you, you know.'

'Adam?'

Fern Barrie nodded towards a short, broad-shouldered young man, now walking four or five yards in front of them, deep in conversation with another male student. 'Adam. You remember. My friend from the refectory.'

Her eyes glinted as she said it, a glance flicking towards Alix. Alix felt momentarily the sort of excitement that comes at the start of amusement-park rides: the moment before the tip into weightlessness.

The silver sunlight, high in the south, dazzled her. Alix got out her sunglasses, to cover her hesitation; snapped them open and put them on. They darkened the brilliance of the high white Victorian main buildings, and the reflections from the refectory's modern expanse of plate-glass windows.

'Thanks,' she said flatly, 'but tell him I'm not interested.'

'You're not?' Fern sounded incredulous. 'But he's really cute.'

'I'm not interested in "cute". I'm not interested, full stop.' Alix heard the acidity of her tone, and apologised. 'Sorry. I've had too much crap from men at the moment. I'm sure your Adam is very nice, but . . .' She shrugged. 'I'm not in the market for a date.'

'Oh, wow,' the brown-haired girl breathed. 'But you look *so* good – that's such a waste!'

Alix snuffled back a giggle. She caught the younger woman's bewildered expression, decided that Fern had been speaking with naive honesty, and went off into smothered laughter again. She found herself responding to the warm spring sunshine; realised that, for the first time in months, she felt physically relaxed, all her muscles untightening.

'It's very nice of you to say so,' she managed, at last. 'Thanks for the compliment.'

'Oh, well . . .' Fern shrugged. The movement of her narrow shoulders lifted her breasts in her tight white T-shirt. Her waist was narrow, the T-shirt lifting out of it and disclosing a strip of pale skin above her belt. 'I speak as I find, like my nan used to say. Hey, why don't you come back to our place? Yannis Road is a tip – well, there's five of us sharing – but there's some coffee somewhere, and you could, like, talk to Adam a bit. I know he wants to talk to *you* . . .'

On the brink of saying no, Alix impulsively thought to herself: *Don't be such a crabby cow! For once in your life, Alix Neville, go have a good time . . .*

'Thanks,' Alix said. 'I will. Shall I follow your bike?

My car's over there. But,' she added, 'I don't want to give your friend the wrong idea. I'm not interested in men right now.'

The young woman swung the heel of her engineer boot in the gravel, crunching the fragments of stone, and looked up under long dark lashes to catch Alix's gaze.

'Or women?' Fern murmured, with a twinkle.

She abruptly straightened up, swung the leather jacket off her shoulder and dragged it on, and trotted off towards her bike, shouting over her shoulder, 'SW18 – I'll race you!'

'But I—' *don't know where you live!*

Never mind!

The rough spring wind ruffled her hair as she broke into a trot, jogging across the courtyard towards the Audi, welcoming, for once, the hiss of breath in her lungs and the beat of blood in her veins. She slammed down on to the upholstery, smelling the rich odour of leather in the car's warmth, and keyed the ignition at the same time as she slammed the door.

'At least this is more exciting than the crowd back at the office!' she muttered, swinging the big car around in a gravel-spraying curve and cutting up two vans on the main road as she exited behind Fern Barrie's bike. She couldn't help the grin on her face.

Not women, either?

Are you sure? she questioned herself, cutting across another car at a roundabout, swaying sideways with a tight corner, and pressing down on the accelerator to keep Fern's bike in sight. *She's cute – cuter than her boyfriend, if it comes to that.*

But she was just joking. That's all. I've seen her: she flirts with *everybody*.

The throb of the Audi's powerful engine vibrated

through her thighs and ass, warming her cunt. A breath caught in her suddenly dry throat.

Even if I did want to, I wouldn't say. She'd be too kind to laugh at me . . . and pity's always worse.

'Alix, I'm *sick* of you moaning!'

'What?' Interrupted mid-speech, Alix lifted her head where she sprawled on her back on the four-seater sofa – the shared house at Yannis Road had a very large front room. She flexed her bare toes, where a patch of sunlight fell on to them. The file of papers on her stomach slipped, and she grabbed at it, rescuing the printout with her scribbled annotations. 'Accelerated course' meant, it seemed, a practical test a week: minimum. She hadn't been paying attention to the work.

'I *said*, I'm fed up of you moaning all the time!' Fern looked up from the mirror that she had placed on the book-piled dining table, and waved the mascara stick in her fingers. 'Either you want to go out with a man, or you don't – I mean, shit or get off the pot, woman!'

A little stiffly, Alix said, 'Sorry. I didn't realise I'd mentioned it that often.'

'Only every day for three weeks . . .'

The young woman abandoned the mascara, picked up a plum lipstick, and coloured her thin-lipped generous mouth with two swipes of colour. It didn't suit her, Alix saw. *Another couple of years and she won't wear that colour with her skin.*

Alix reached down and heaved herself up into a sitting position on the soft sofa, letting the hardcopies of the programs slide every which way. 'Maybe I'd better go back to the flat.'

An altercation broke out in the kitchen, loud enough for both of them to hear Adam protesting, and another of the sharing students, Robbie, replying. Fern Barrie grinned. 'I'd better go sort that out. No, don't go – I've got something for you. Hang on!'

Alix bent down, feeling under the edge of the sofa for her trainers. She slipped them on to her bare feet, not bothering to undo the laces. For a moment, she stared at her reflection in the patio window – loose, tousled silver-blonde hair, a lipstick-pink T-shirt with a scooped neckline that showed a shadowed cleavage, and cut-off blue jeans made into the sort of shorts that the middle of May demands. She stretched one bare leg, watching the sheen of the light on her skin.

I'm turning into a student, she realised, amused. Turning the clock back. Hell, I don't look any older than most of this lot . . .

'That's taken their minds off *that*!' Fern bounced back into the room. She dusted her hands down the short, straight skirt she was wearing. An injured silence hung behind her, and the subdued sound of male students making inroads on piles of dirty crockery. 'Oh, hey, look: *this* is what I was saving for you!'

Despite herself, Alix smiled and reached out to take the sheet of paper the younger woman was holding out to her. 'What's this? Umm . . . what *is* this?'

Fern sat down, straddling the arm of the sofa, her short black skirt riding up her thighs. What Alix had taken to be pantyhose were, in fact, stockings; the tab of one suspender was just visible. The tatty old sweatshirt hanging over the skirt argued a great deal more dressing-up before the going-out phase might be reached.

'It's genuine,' Fern said. 'I checked at the office. Professor Mayhew's the one that wrote those books. She was on TV.'

Alix smoothed the crumpled paper over her knee.

She could feel the warmth of Fern's silk-covered thigh, close to, but not touching, her own upper arm. She licked her suddenly dry lips, and concentrated on the writing in front of her:

> Psychology professor seeks volunteers for experimental programme; interviews Friday 18th. Contact V. Mayhew, c/o the Student Union office. No time-wasters, please.

'Is that *Vivienne* Mayhew?' Alix said slowly. 'She wrote *Hidden Pleasure*, and – what was it? I forget the name of the second one. Oh, yeah – *Under Covers*. I didn't realise she was teaching at Pardoe College. She comes across as more of a TV personality than an academic...'

Alix had picked up the book-of-the-programme, a ground-breaking study of women's sexual fantasies. She had read a couple of pages in the bookshop, and – slightly pink – taken it straight to the cash desk.

'*Hidden Pleasure* was good,' she admitted. 'Wasn't that a few years ago, though?'

'Dunno.' Fern's sharp-nailed hand stabbed down at the paper. As she leaned over Alix, Alix felt the full strength of her overpowering perfume. 'Who cares? She's doing this now.'

'Doesn't say much about it...'

'No. It wouldn't, would it?' Fern leaned back, kicking her heel against the floor. 'I'm going on Friday. Adam's not coming, but Robbie is, if he doesn't chicken out. Are you going to come too?'

'Me?'

'You!' Fern gave her a wicked grin. 'Boring old you. Come *on*, Alix. Whatever it is, it'll be fun. It's got to be about sex!'

Alix bent down and picked up her papers, shuffling them together and squaring the edges of the pile.

'No,' she said at last. 'No, it does sound interesting, but . . . no. Not for me.'

A week later, with the latest test safely (if tardily) handed in, Alix stopped at the mail office to check her pigeon-hole. There was rarely much there: she did not intend to join student organisations, or attend sports outings, during this brief sabbatical from her career.

This time, there was a single sheet of paper, in a brown envelope. Curious, she ripped it open.

Will the following volunteers please contact Professor Mayhew to arrange their first interviews for the programme:

Skimming down, Alix caught sight of Fern's name among the list of students otherwise unknown to her. She grinned. The expression faded as she saw a stripe of yellow highlighter swiped boldly across one name:

ALIX NEVILLE.

'What!'

Her breath caught, dry in her throat, and a stab of adrenalin went through her body. She found she was standing with one hand in a fist, pressed to her solar plexus. Anger fanned itself into a flame, making her cheeks heat and redden.

Out loud, she shouted, '*Fern*!'

Alix tracked the girl down to the refectory. This time, when she entered, it was packed full of students. The sound of conversation was deafening, bouncing back off the undecorated brick walls. An odour of cooking suffused the air. All the windows stood open, to counteract it. And by the end window, at a table with Adam and Robbie and an older blonde girl whose name Alix still didn't know, Fern Barrie sat.

Alix shoved her way between the crowded tables. It was noisy enough that she had to raise her voice, even with her hand on the back of Fern's chair. 'I want a word with you!'

The brown-haired girl leaned back. Her wide mouth was pressed shut. Alix couldn't tell if she were stifling a grin or an expression of irritation. Alix slapped the envelope down on the table in front of her, among Coke cans and sandwich wrappers.

'This is you, isn't it!'

The young woman quickly licked her fingers, pink tongue darting, and swallowed the last of her sandwich. She reached out and unfolded the sheet of paper.

'Oh. Yeah. That's me.'

'Why the *hell* did you think you could do—?'

'Alix!' Fern cut her off.

Breathing heavily, Alix stopped speaking. She stared down at the tiny woman.

'Alix,' Fern Barrie said again, 'I've got one thing to say to you. *Get over yourself*. Okay, so I signed up for the project under my name *and* under yours – Joley here did the interview for you. It was with one of the professor's research students, so Professor Mayhew won't know it wasn't you. Now all you have to do is turn up whenever your appointment is. It's all yours.'

'I don't want it!'

'Don't say that,' the blonde whose name turned out to be Joley murmured, in what seemed to be a habitually quiet voice. Alix had to bend down to catch what she added. 'You don't know what it is yet . . .'

'No,' Alix said grimly, 'I don't. I *do* know I'm too old for student pranks.'

As if she hadn't spoken, Fern shifted around in the seat to look up at her. She curled her feet underneath herself, pixie-like, boots scraping against the edge of the wooden chair.

'It's cool,' she announced. 'It's *really* cool. You know what Professor Mayhew wants?'

I don't care what Professor Mayhew wants!

'Something to do with sexual fantasies again, I presume,' Alix said, coolly.

'Women's sexual fantasies,' Fern confirmed. 'First, anyway. Tough luck on Adam and Robbie here . . .'

The stocky Adam, head down, muttered something embarrassed. Robbie echoed Fern's grin, his own regretful under the thin, half-shaved beard he wore.

'So it's another book like *Hidden Pleasure*—' Alix's irritation faded a little.

Another book, which I wouldn't mind reading. Would it really be so bad to have to write down what turns me on? I guess that Professor Mayhew would disguise the names again . . .

'Not *just* like *Hidden Pleasure*,' Fern said, eyes bright. 'You wait till you hear this, Alix. This is her next big academic project. She's already studied the sexual fantasies that women have . . .'

The small brunette's voice dropped to a whisper, too soft to be heard by anybody more than a foot away. Alix had to bend lower, catching the warm waft of perfume from Fern's body.

'What she wants to study this time . . . it's how many women are willing, when it comes to it, to put their sexual fantasies into *practice*.'

Chapter Three

'*I'VE COME TO TELL* you to take me off your list,' Alix said abruptly.

Professor Vivienne Mayhew looked up from the monitor screen. Her luxurious dark hair swung back from her face. It hung down to her shoulders. She swivelled her chair round, in the tiny office, so that she faced Alix.

'Yes?' The sunlight from the old-fashioned sash window showed faint lines at the corners of her large, dark eyes. The slightest of creases marked a line at the corners of her mouth. She must be forty, forty-five. Her figure, evidently once slim, had a slight softness of line about it now.

And then, as she leaned back in the swivel chair, a sudden lazy elegance took years off her. 'And you'll be. . . ?'

Startled, Alix realised there was no reason for her to be known to the woman. 'Alix. Alix Neville.'

'Ah . . . yes . . .' Professor Mayhew's slender fingers rattled on the computer keyboard. Her skin was olive, reflecting the warmth of her delicate gold rings. A list of names flashed up on the screen.

Alix caught sight of her own reflection in the curved

glass. Her face had an anxious, tight expression.

'Here you are. "Alix Neville". My assistant gave you a "recommended" rating – although she doesn't seem to have many of your personal details down . . .'

Vivienne Mayhew's voice was soft, deep, with the rasp of a ragged edge to it. Maybe she had smoked in her youth, Alix thought; imagining the woman in a university, in the 1970s, with punk make-up, perhaps? She smiled at the thought. There was no doubt why the woman worked on TV. Professorial, sexy and intelligent; all in one dark-haired, womanly, photogenic package . . .

Am I *jealous*? Alix thought, suddenly. Because I have a boring job in an office, and she—

'I'm a bit older than the rest of your students,' she said, interrupting her own unwelcome thoughts. 'It'd probably throw your calculations off, or something. Anyway, it's not really me. So . . .'

'Do sit down, Alix.' The woman waved, invitingly, to a stuffed brown armchair crammed into a corner of the room. A set of bookshelves threatened to overflow on to it. Many were paperbacks, the spines thoroughly cracked. 'Let's have a coffee, shall we?'

'Well, I . . .' It seemed suddenly impolite to reject that calm, kind, non-threatening gaze. Gingerly, Alix seated herself on the edge of the sagging armchair. She sank down into it. The hem of her blue cotton shift-dress tightened as it rode up her bare thighs. She tugged ineffectually at it.

'Coffee's instant, I'm afraid.' Vivienne stood, not needing to do more than turn around on the spot and switch on the kettle, which was on top of a filing cabinet. She stood up on her toes, smooth stockinged heels sliding up out of her black court shoes. Her ankles were delicately curved. As she rummaged in the cupboard above, her muffled voice added: 'It would be useful if you could tell me what objections you've developed to the programme, since your interview . . . I won't use anything without your permission, of course . . . Ah, *there* we are.'

She rested back into her low-heeled shoes, slightly breathless. She held a jar of coffee triumphantly in her hand. Absently, she smoothed down her black linen skirt over her curved hips with her free hand. She ran a thumb around under the waistband, settling her cream silk blouse. The heat of the sun on the window had brought a slight moist dampness to the silk, Alix saw, and it heightened the musky fragrance of her perfume.

'I just don't fancy doing it any more,' Alix said flatly.

'It's understandable that you might be nervous, but you seemed so keen in the interview . . .'

Damn Joley! Damn Fern!

'. . . And if I don't have a certain number of women, the survey becomes statistically meaningless.' Vivienne Mayhew turned, passing Alix a very full bright red mug with the tips of her elegant fingers. Taking her own steaming cup, she seated herself again and leaned forward, looking into Alix's face. 'Not that that should bother you, my dear. To begin with, it's not your problem, and to end with, one volunteer is worth ten pressed men. Or women.'

The coffee mug was hot enough to burn Alix's fingers. She set it down carefully on the bare, stained floorboards. Accepting it, she realised, had obligated her to stay here until she could drink it – *Professor Mayhew isn't stupid, is she*?

She looked again at the dark-haired woman. The lines of Vivienne Mayhew's bra straps were faintly visible under the cream blouse, and between the couple of undone buttons the famous cleavage looked rather less impressive than on TV. But still, the woman was radiating sexual appeal, all unconsciously.

And that's what I'm jealous of, Alix thought. The confidence. If someone turns her down, she'll just think 'their problem'!

I was like that, once.

'It's not that I haven't done things,' Alix protested hastily.

' "Things"?' the woman enquired delicately.

'I was into heavy SM, once . . . top and bottom.' A memory made Alix's cheeks heat up. She looked down at the glistening liquid in her coffee mug. 'A few years ago. So, you see, it's not nerves.'

'No . . .' There was only the slightest hint in Professor Mayhew's tone that could imply a question. Alix could see how people would respond to her.

Because she comes across as trustworthy. She never did disclose her sources for *Hidden Pleasure*, did she? She seems . . . safe.

'It's good that *somebody*'s doing this,' Alix said. She pointed at copies of the book on the Professor's shelves. 'Somebody should . . .'

'Why *not* you?' Vivienne Mayhew said incisively.

Alix opened her mouth to answer. A sudden cold sweat dampened her back, under her T-shirt. Her palms sweated. Changing her mind, she blurted out, 'It wasn't me at the interview!'

'At the . . . Not you? Then who was it?'

'It was Joley. That's a friend of a friend of mine. Well. I *thought* she was a friend.' Alix didn't look up from the coils of vapour rising up from the coffee mug on the floorboards. Sunlight striped the wood and the warm colour of the ceramic. 'It was never anything to do with me, I didn't volunteer, I didn't want to do it – I just forgot what nineteen-year-olds can be like. I'm sorry they've messed you about.'

There was a pause. She looked up. Vivienne Mayhew's gaze was absent, staring into unseen thoughts. The dark brown eyes snapped back into focus, suddenly, pinning Alix in her gaze.

'I repeat,' Vivienne said, 'why *not* you?'

'But . . .'

A sharp knock was followed instantly by the door opening. Without waiting for any comment, a tall, sharp-faced man barged through into the room, and stabbed one finger at Professor Mayhew.

'Vivienne, *what* am I to make of this? The girl is one of my best students. I won't have you taking up her time with this unhealthy nonsense!'

He hesitated, as his narrowed eyes met Alix's. She saw him realise that there was another person in the room, that it was a student, that it was female.

Without hesitation, the man went on: 'I can't spare her, you must know that!'

Vivienne Mayhew spoke. 'Who are we talking about, Jordan?' She leaned back in her swivel chair, not rising to her feet to attempt to tower over him – which would have been difficult, Alix saw: the newcomer must have been six foot, six foot one. In his dark suit, with such dark hair, he seemed all sharp edges.

'Fern Barrie, of course! Who else of my students is capable of scoring over 95 per cent in a philosophy test?'

Alix felt her mouth drop open. About to say *Fern*! in tones of utter incredulity, she shut her lips firmly together. *Who is this pain in the ass, anyway?*

'I'm afraid I don't agree with your assessment, Professor Axley,' Vivienne Mayhew said, formally. The openness that had been in her face while she spoke to Alix vanished. She watched Axley through eyes veiled with long, dark lashes. 'This project will only occupy the students' spare time—'

'As if they didn't spend enough time thinking about sex as it is!' the Professor said, distaste plain in his tone. 'Now you want them to think about it, write it down for you – it *isn't* healthy! I want them studying Kant and Hume, not scribbling down their wet dreams so that you can publish them!'

Alix felt her face flush. Then her temper went from anger to amazement in a breath. She realised: *He thinks it's another book of* written *fantasies, nothing more – has he got a shock coming!* She leaned back in the saggy armchair, looking up at the man – Jordan Axley? – with a sense almost of pleasure.

I didn't know dinosaurs like him existed any more. And he can't be more than thirty, thirty-five . . . He ought to be preserved in a museum. Labelled *Young Fogey*!

'Thank you for your input, Professor Axley,' Vivienne Mayhew said gently. Her generous lips curved in a smile. One hand went up to her hair, where it tumbled in brown and ebony coils over her shoulders. 'You can, of course, take it up with the Head of Department at the next meeting . . .'

Nicest *Fuck off*! I've ever heard, Alix thought, barely keeping a grin off her face.

A hand rapped on the door frame. She heard a deep voice, with the trace of an American accent, as the man put his head around the open door. 'Anybody home? Oh, Jordan, hi. Vivienne, it was you I wanted to see – those attendance records . . .'

'Sandro, come in; I have them for you here.' Vivienne Mayhew sounded as though she welcomed the interruption.

There was barely room for three of them in the tiny

office, and the newcomer made it even more crowded. His size made it seem a cluttered cupboard of a room.

Alix thought, *That accent's East Coast*. The sagging armchair prevented her getting easily to her feet. She leaned forward to get a look at him.

You're never an academic!

Any bigger and his size would have made him a bear of a man – a Viking, she thought, gazing up at his short, corn-yellow hair. As it was, he was long-legged and loose-limbed; tall in proportion to his weight. He wore a faded white cotton sweatshirt, stretching tight across his pecs. A sprinkling of gold-wire chest hairs showed under his collar. He wore trainers and jeans. He looked way too young to be a member of staff, but too old to be a student – her own age, give or take a year either way, she thought.

Looking up gave her a crick in her neck. As the newcomer said something to Jordan Axley, she lowered her gaze.

Of necessity in the tiny office, the man stood crammed in next to the brown armchair, beside her. His blue jeans were so faded they were almost white. A sudden erotic charge sparked along Alix's nerves. She knew without touching how smooth and soft the worn denim would feel. How hot and hard and muscular the body under it ... With her in the low armchair, she found herself sitting with her head at the level of his hips, and looking straight at the bulge of his crotch behind the soft material. She flushed, the breath catching in her throat. She wanted to reach out and lay the hot, sweating palm of her hand against that bulge; feel it move and leap in response. She wondered what it would feel like to put her hand down his pants.

Alix looked away, embarrassed by the strength of her own reaction. She was still conscious of his long muscular legs beside her. With an effort, she started to get to her feet, too intimidated to sit so far below his eye level.

'... *And* these files,' Vivienne Mayhew finished, heaving a stack of manila folders from the far side of her desk.

The blond man fumbled the folders as he took them, almost spilling papers on the floor. Alix automatically reached out to help. His hands caught the pile, without her assistance; swept the folders back together – sun-brown hands, with broad fingers and small scars and abrasions on the knuckles.

Even standing, she was a head shorter than him.

Oh wow, Alix thought. She studied his face, animated while he spoke to Professor Mayhew. He had been out in the sun. Squint lines marked the corners of his eyes, pale against his tan. She could see him sailing, maybe, on a yacht around the Greek Islands ... or exercising horses, perhaps; or anything out-of-doors.

Who am I kidding? He's a graduate student or a junior member of staff. He spends about as much time in the Great Outdoors as I do. Just because he *looks* like a cowboy ...

She looked him in the face, to see brilliant dark blue eyes regarding her with utter coolness.

'You don't agree with this, surely?' Professor Axley snapped.

The blond man lifted one shoulder in a supremely indifferent shrug. 'We should have some, ah, record of female sexuality, I guess.'

Maybe he's embarrassed? Alix wondered. *Is that it?* She straightened, letting her weight go back on her rear foot and lifting her head. She knew the sun was behind her, that it would show up her long silvery hair to its best advantage. The light blue cotton shift-dress she was wearing would show off her breasts and hips ... but not as much as if I'd dressed up, she thought.

She lifted her gaze, looked at him from under her long lashes and gave him her best cool smile.

His blue eyes flicked away from her without interest.

Oh no, not another one! Not another creep that I have to get the hots for—!

Or does he think I'm a student, and he's a member of staff, and therefore he *can't* show any interest? That's easily fixed.

'Hi,' she said brightly, ignoring Vivienne Mayhew's curious glance. 'I'm Alix Neville. My company sent me along to do your advanced computer-security module.'

'Nice for you,' the man said flatly.

He could not, Alix thought, have shown greater lack of interest if he'd ignored her completely. She opened her mouth to make a snappy comeback but couldn't think of one.

'Sandro's over here on his sabbatical year.' Professor Mayhew smoothed over the awkward silence. 'Alix Neville: Sandro Elliot. Sandro's helping us out while he finishes his book on late-Victorian gender roles.'

'A man's take on a woman's subject.' Sandro Elliot's voice remained cold, and he stared down at Alix as if daring her to contradict him. She wanted to see him smile, see some warmth in his expression, some response to her friendliness. There was nothing. He looked away from her. 'Thanks, Professor Mayhew. Jordan ...'

The dark man burst out, 'But this is ridiculous! It's completely unacademic—'

Vivienne Mayhew turned a smouldering look on Axley. The tone of her voice remained level. 'Sexuality is a perfectly viable field of academic study, Jordan. Knowing what proportion of the population get erotic satisfaction from being tied up, helpless, and masturbated to a climax, is no less a key to human nature than Hume's and Descartes' theories.'

Alix saw the dark-haired man shift uncomfortably from one foot to the other. A glistening film of sweat shone on his forehead. Struck by an idea, she looked down. A faint bulge was pushing out the front of his trousers.

So, the Professor likes hearing about people being tied up. Does he want to be tied, or do the tying, though? He'd make a good top . . .

Axley snapped, 'And my students have to waste their time with *this*?'

'Yes,' Vivienne Mayhew said. Alix saw the tip of her tongue lick at her lower lip and a faint smile pulling at her mouth. 'All the while it makes Pardoe College well known, yes, I get to carry on my work here.'

'*Work!*' With a look that Alix thought could have melted through a plate-glass window, Jordan Axley turned and stalked off through the doorway, shouldering his way past Sandro Elliot.

'What's biting his ass?' Elliot murmured.

As he turned to look at the departing Jordan Axley, Alix found herself staring at his neat buns, and the triangular body-line that ran up from his hips to his shoulders. She let her gaze slide over the soft cloth of his shirt, imagining how his muscled back would feel to the touch. And her gaze moved back down, inevitably, to the worn leather belt in the loops of his faded jeans, and his taut buttocks under the soft denim.

Oh man, but he's sex on legs! What is it about me – why doesn't he want to know?

Vivienne Mayhew said, 'Some men are threatened by female sexuality. Strange, though. I always thought Jordan wasn't interested in anything female.'

'Maybe he just doesn't want to hear about their hot fantasies, Professor.' A flicker of something like distaste passed over Elliot's sun-lined features. At the same time that she wanted to hit him, Alix wanted to run her fingertips over his cheek, and see if she could feel the first trace of after-shaving stubble.

'Could be pressure on him?' he added, enigmatically. 'Thanks again, Professor Mayhew. See you 'round.'

He did not look at Alix or say goodbye to her. The door clicked shut behind him in a potent silence.

'What is it about me?' Alix exclaimed. 'Do I smell? Should I go around with a paper bag over my head? Is he gay?'

Vivienne Mayhew gave a rich, gurgling chuckle. She smiled at Alix. 'No, he's not the latter. I've not known him be short on female company since he arrived.'

'That's no excuse for looking at me like I'm a dead fish!'

A tinge of the familiar depression stole over her. This time, it sparked a feeling of irritation – with Sandro Elliot, with all the men of the last twelve months. Mainly, with herself.

Dammit, he's got no right!

'Tell me about this project,' she demanded. 'Fern will do anything for a laugh, and I didn't pay much attention to her. What exactly is it that you're doing here?'

Slowly and elegantly, like a cat returning to a favoured seat, Vivienne Mayhew sank down on to her office chair. She picked up her cooling cup of coffee.

'Testing the limits of fantasy, I suppose,' she said. 'I want to know how many women who have a favourite sexual fantasy are prepared to try for the same satisfaction in real life. It'll be another book, when I'm finished. An analysis of the differences and similarities between masturbatory fantasies and the real-life experience of those same fantasies. If you want to have sex with a man in public, say, and you fantasise about that and you come – will you come, in real life, with real onlookers, or is that not what the erotic charge of it is about?'

Alix swallowed, aware of how dry her mouth was. A piercing ache went through her cleft as she shifted from one foot to the other. Still standing, she looked down at Vivienne Mayhew. 'So how does it work? We tell you what the fantasy is—'

'I get you to write it down. A few sentences, it doesn't need to be much.'

'—Okay, write it down, and then . . .'

'Within the limits of safety,' the other woman said, 'we support you to live out your fantasy in real life. Then you write another short piece, saying which was best – the reality or the fantasy. Or if both were "best", in different ways. Or neither.'

Alix said nothing for a long minute.

'How many have you had so far?' she said at last.

'We're just starting. You would be the fifth. I'm . . .' The luscious brunette woman flushed, colour rising up her smooth neck and cheeks. 'I'm writing down one of mine, as a helpful guideline. Of course, you can always borrow my books to see how other women have written theirs. Literary style doesn't matter. Pleasure is what matters.'

Alix said sourly, 'Listen, you might as well know, fantasy's all I've had for quite a while.'

'That's good.' Vivienne smiled. 'I mean, it's good that you have that. Prolonged celibacy without sexual fantasy . . . you get used to being without it. The body shuts down. That sexual theatre in the mind is our way of keeping the body turned on and finely tuned. It's a lover that never lets you down.'

'But in real life . . .'

'That's what I'm researching. Are things always better as fantasy? Isn't it possible that the women who have the courage to put their fantasies into practice are the ones who are more fulfilled?'

'And if you were a man,' Alix said, staring through the open door at the passage down which Sandro Elliot had vanished, 'you wouldn't need to ask. Some specialist sex-worker would already have let you find out . . . "Gender roles"!'

'Oh, Sandro's not a bad man.' The older woman smiled.

A rude shit is a rude shit, here or in the States. How dare he ignore me like that? Does he walk in to work over a road full of prostrate, willing bimbos?

Despite herself, she chuckled at the mental picture.

'You sound as though you're considering being a part of the project,' Vivienne Mayhew said carefully.

'Maybe . . .' Alix looked up. 'Maybe I'm just thinking of a question my friend Lew asked me at work. He asked me how long since I'd enjoyed sex. Too long, that's the answer. Too long.'

'If he could ask that question,' Vivienne said, 'perhaps you should be going out with him instead of doing this? He sounds a good man.'

'Oh, he is,' Alix agreed. 'He is . . . That's why he's got a girlfriend he won't dump. He says they have an open relationship and she brings home other women for them, but I don't know if that's just his fantasy – probably not, actually. He sounds like he knows what he's talking about.' She hesitated. 'I suppose the real ideal would be to have a relationship too, and explore your fantasies with that person, wouldn't it?'

'Sadly, we can't provide you with a partner like that.'

'No, I don't suppose that does come with the programme!'

'So . . . ?' Vivienne prompted.

'So . . .' Alix took a deep breath. 'What do you need to know about me?'

'A few details – number of sexual partners, the last time you had sex with a man, or a woman; frequency of self-pleasuring . . .' Vivienne raised a beautifully shaped brow. 'Does this mean . . .'

Again, that top-of-the-rollercoaster feeling. And this time I'm taking the trip! Alix thought. She smiled, with the first tinges of real excitement.

'Count me in,' she said.

Chapter Four

ALIX WASN'T CONSCIOUS OF much else until she found herself standing outside the main college building, a chilled can of soft drink in her hand. She snapped the tab and tilted the can to her lips, swallowing. The fizzy liquid cut through her slight dizziness. The coldness of it was welcome under the hot May sunshine.

Am I really going to. . . ?

Well, yes, I am. I suppose I'd better think about what I'm going to write down for Vivienne.

The campus buildings stretched off in all directions. Too wound up to go back to her car and back to the empty flat, she turned and walked off at random. Her steps led her towards the wide, green lawns beyond the Victorian main building. The scent of newly cut grass filled her nostrils.

She stopped on the tarmac path, and stretched her arms up and outwards. The sunlight fell warm on her skin. A slight shiver of goosepimples followed. White clouds sailed overhead, pushed by the occasional breeze. She could hear a tugboat siren, out on the distant river Thames.

Well ... There was that time I went to an SM club ...

Her skin seemed to become utterly sensitive at the thought. The thin fabric of her dress slid softly over her thighs as the wind caught it. The slight abrasion made her nipples peak up, taut against the fine cotton.

'But that's not what I want,' she said to herself, under her breath. 'Not now, anyway ...'

What have *I been fantasising about, recently? Other than a man who doesn't treat me like dirt?*

Alix shifted the strap of her bag on her shoulder, aware suddenly that she had walked to the edge of one of the wide college lawns. A great cedar tree occupied the middle of the grass. The green branches swept down, almost to the ground, heavily laden with clumps of needles. A slight tang of resin flavoured the air. The alternately swelling and receding sound of a lawnmower came distantly to her.

She bent down, hooked off her sandals, and stepped barefoot on to the cut green grass. It prickled softly between her toes. The sun had warmed it: there was no trace of damp. Careful of fir cones, she picked her way across the lawn and ducked under the trailing branches of the cedar tree.

Here, shadows and sunlight mottled the earth. Grass grew sparsely, overlaid with a carpet of brown needles. A few chocolate-bar wrappers made it apparent this was a favourite student hang-out, but no one was present at the moment.

Alix sank down, her back to the trunk of the cedar tree. She fumbled through her bag for a notebook and pencil. The drooping branches swayed above her, creaking. Sunlight and shadow by turns brightened and dimmed the white page in front of her.

What should I write?

She sucked at the top of the pencil. Her lipstick

smudged the shaft. Tetchy, she thumbed it clean, and leaned back against the rough bark, gazing upwards. The hum of the mower came closer. A powered motor, engine noise thrumming on the air – one of the vehicle-type ones you sit on, she realised. She lowered her gaze to see the gardener driving up and down the lawns, where they ran down towards the river, coming gradually closer to the cedar. Some old guy striping the lawns dark and pale green.

Maybe somebody who just can't resist me – who has to have me . . .

The breeze found its way under the branches and licked at her cheek. It blew her hair back from her face to tickle her bare shoulders. And it cooled her feet on the pine needles, and her legs where she sat with her dress rucked up.

There was no one around, except the distant lawn-mower driver. She drew her legs up and put her arms around her knees. The notebook and pencil slid down, unnoticed. The warm wind caressed the undersides of her bare thighs and her crotch, where her dress pulled up to expose her cream silk knickers.

She felt every baby-soft hair on her skin responding to the moving air. Slowly, she let one hand dip between her thighs. Her eyes closed. The pad of her middle finger slid over the silky material at her crotch, feeling the heat underneath. Eyes still shut, she slid her finger under the gusset of her panties, into the wet heat, stroking the swollen aching flesh there. A surge of wanting went through her cunt. She began to stroke, sliding her finger between her labia, smoothing her hot juices up and over her clit. The nub of flesh almost hurt with the pent-up desire for release.

She became aware that the sound of the mower had stopped.

Footsteps rustling on the fallen needles warned her of someone's presence.

Her eyes snapped open. In one swift movement, she shoved herself up on to her feet, dragged her dress down, and seized her college bag. Her face burned red. She took two steps away, found herself barefoot on fir needles again, and swore. Grabbing her sandal up and clasping it in her hand, she staggered out through the cedar's swooping branches into the open.

'Miss—'

Alix stopped. Her chest heaved. The sun shone blindingly hard now, down from a noon sky. The only people visible were hundreds of yards away: mere coloured dots in the distance. She turned around on the soft, trimmed grass.

The man standing under the tree was the gardener, she realised. The one who had been sitting on the motor-mower. He was not an old man – he'd looked bald from a distance, but in fact he was shaven-headed, and young. The machine rested a few paces away from the cedar now.

'You forgot your other shoe,' he said.

'Oh – thanks.'

Alix didn't move. She waited. He stepped out from under the shadows of the tree.

The sun blazed back from his fair hair, shaved close to his scalp, and from his bare shoulders and arms and chest. He didn't look much more than twenty-five. He wore old denim jeans, marked with earth and spatters of paint. A faded shirt hung over the back of the seat of the mower. Where he held her sandal, it looked tiny in his rough, sunburned hand.

She waited, making him come forward. Her chin lifted as he did. He was taller than her, and his chest was a golden-brown tan. His arms were rounded with muscle. His chest was smooth, all but hairless. She breathed in as he stood close to her, smelling warmth and masculine sweat.

Below his belt there was a bulge at the fly of his jeans. She felt suddenly that she wanted just to reach out and grab his neat hips, and pull his body close to her...

'You were watching me,' she said. Her voice stayed calm, not accusing.

A smile tilted his mouth. He put his hand across the stubble on his head and surveyed her through clear green eyes. 'You weren't objecting.'

'I didn't know!'

'Aw, c'mon; you musta known *some*one would look at that...' His gaze dropped from her face to her crotch. She felt herself getting hot.

She licked at her dry lips. 'What's your name?'

'Tom.'

There was nothing – nothing – in his expression, she realised, except fierce desire. No contempt, no triumph. Just plain lust.

And lust is always a compliment, isn't it?

'Okay, Tom... why don't you take me for a ride... on your mower?'

He looked startled for a second, gazing from her to the machine and back. She grinned. One glance went towards the college buildings. No one in sight. He wiped his wrist across his sweating face, paused for a moment, and then grinned back at her.

'Sure,' he said.

He turned and walked towards the lawnmower. Alix began to walk after him. Her legs felt like jelly. She glanced down and saw that her hands were shaking – the tremor of desire. As the man reached the machine and turned back, his gaze raked her from head to foot.

His frank admiration made her nipples stiffen and her cunt wet.

'There's only a seat for one,' he said.

'Have to sit on your lap then, won't I?' She hooked her bag and sandals over the back of the seat, and stood waiting expectantly. Sweat dampened her underarms. A trickle of it ran from her forehead down her chin to her neck, and slid under the neck of her dress, and down between her breasts.

The man, Tom, stood watching her for a minute. The front of his work jeans bulged. Awkwardly, he climbed up on to the seat of the mower, kicking the engine into life. The deep *thrum* vibrated through the earth: she felt it through her bare feet. I can still turn back, she thought.

But I don't want to. So I'm not going to.

'Take me for a ride!' Alix demanded.

She swung herself up on to the motor-mower and landed rather more solidly than she'd planned in Tom's lap. He grunted. Her buttocks hit his thighs. She wriggled herself back, pushing her back into his belly and parting her legs a little. The thrust of his cock under her made her gasp. She felt it clearly through the material of his trousers.

'Oh, man . . .' he groaned in her ear. His breath feathered warm and moist against the skin of her neck. One of his hands came up and buried itself in her hair, his rough-skinned fingers catching at the silver strands.

His other hand shifted gears and let the motor roar. The mower began to move. At low gear it vibrated heavily. She felt the vibration through her thighs, her labia, her clit, her inner muscles. *Like riding a giant vibrator* – she smiled at the thought.

As the machine moved, Alix felt her bum moving against his body: the hardness of his muscled thighs, the swelling thrust of his cock. His other arm came around her stomach, clasping her back against his bare chest. The sun-warmed, tanned flesh of his body glued itself to her.

'Wow . . .' he breathed. She let her head fall back, resting it against his collarbone. The motor-mower bucked under them. His bulging crotch pressed up against hers, lifting her off the seat, so that she was riding high above the ground as they rumbled along. His hand clamped suddenly hard over her left breast.

'Ah—!' She let herself relax into it. His strong fingers kneaded at her breast through her dress. Almost pain: a strong pleasure. She thrust herself forward, into his hand. Reading the movement he moved his hand back for a second, then plunged it down the front of her dress, grabbing a fistful of warm breast. Her skin shivered and her nipple jutted out hard. His fingers dug in sharply enough to leave their imprint on her pale skin.

'Oh, yes . . .' she breathed. A sudden unevenness in the ground made the vehicle judder. She dropped her hand to her lap, hitching up her skirt. With the pads of her fingers she pressed against the warm crotch of her panties, over her clitoris. Hot liquid soaked through the material. She felt the folds of her labia swelling and opening like a rose.

His hand left her dress and closed over hers in her lap. It pressed down, forcing her against the swollen hot erection in his pants. His breath gasped in her ear, warm and wet. Helpless between his hips and his hand, she let her head go back and her body relax into the juddering shiver of pre-orgasm.

'Can't—' he wrenched the wheel over with his free hand, away from a building that had come astonishingly close in a few seconds. 'Not here – people will see—'

'Where? *Where*?'

For an answer, he swung the wheel, bringing the motor-mower around in a half-circle. It began to speed up, juddering off the grass and over gravel now, heading towards the gardeners' yard and sheds. Her body ached with the desire to have something – his fingers, her fingers, his cock, anything – stuffed up her hot cunt. She writhed and squirmed in his lap, thrusting her buttocks back against him. The hem of her dress rode up. She felt his fingers forcing a way between their sweaty bodies and pulling at the back of her knickers. She lifted herself a little, legs trembling. He dragged her silk knickers down over her hips and exposed half her buttocks, pressing himself back against her again. The buckle of his belt jammed into her soft flesh.

'*Where*?' she demanded.

'Here! H-here!'

The vehicle swung into the yard. A high wall cut them off from sight of the college. Alix saw no one in the yard, no one in the sheds and greenhouses—

She found herself lifted, thrust up into the air by his hips and cock, sliding free – and her feet hit the gravel hard. She sank down into a squat, reached out her hands to support herself on the rough ground. Her breath hissed in her throat. She felt dizzy with wanting. She heard his shoes hit the gravel behind her.

'In here! Quick!'

Uncoordinated with desire, she let him put his rough hands under her arms, all but dragging her along. She stumbled, bare feet bitten by the harsh gravel. She barely noticed. They passed one locked shed door – she heard him whimper – and then came to another door. A greenhouse. He reached past her and slid the glass door aside.

'In *here*!'

The door clicked closed behind them. A wave of heat hit her, among the plant trays and shrouding greenery. Sweat sprang out on her face and neck and breasts. She swung around, grabbing for his wrists.

He loomed over her, breath coming hard in his throat. His face was flushed dark red. He grinned, teeth shining white in the green gloom. Spatters of warm condensation fell and rolled down his chest. Still holding his wrists, she leaned over and licked her tongue from his lower ribs to his nipple. His skin tasted hot and salty. He groaned.

'Ah, God, I want you!' He slid his hard, thick wrists easily out of her grip. The scent of herbs filled the hot air. Both his hands came down on her shoulders, grabbed her, slid around to her spine and pressed her tight against the length of his body.

She slid her hands between their bellies. With her prodding fingers, she worked one hand under his belt and under the waistband of his work jeans. He tensed and moved fractionally back. She slipped her hand down into hot darkness and clasped a thick throbbing shaft.

'Oh, the size of that!' she murmured.

He stood further back from her for a second, put his hands to her hips, seized her and lifted her bodily up into the air. She felt her bum come down hard on the wooden bench, plants and seedlings flying. A scatter of warm earth covered her hand where she put it out to support herself. Leaning back on the waist-high bench, she parted her legs and thrust her breasts forward at him.

Both his hands went to his fly. With difficulty, he tugged down his zip, caught over the bulk of his erection. The throbbing cock sprang free – at last – bobbing red and purple and glistening.

She reached out her free hand, closing it round the hot hardness of him. He smelled wonderfully of sex and sweat and heat. Carefully she drew him towards her. His jeans slid down his legs, showing his white thighs and hobbling him. She touched her thumb gently to the underside of his glans. His cock leaped in her hand.

'I *want* you!' His voice sounded rough and uncontrolled. His arms swept the bench clear and he pulled her forward to the edge. Her earth-stained dress rucked up, pulled over her thighs, then her buttocks. He reached down to the front of her belly, knuckles brushing the soft sensitive skin and making her jump. He grabbed the front of her knickers and ripped. The flimsy fabric tore and vanished. 'I want *you*!'

Bare-arsed, she found the heated damp air on her skin deliciously erotic. Her labia throbbed. The ache in her cunt deepened. She let go of him, bracing her hands against the wooden bench. 'Fuck me!'

'You asked for it,' he gasped, 'and you're going to get it!'

His hands seized her hips again, fingertips digging in hard. She felt herself tilted back. The air glided smoothly and sensually across her exposed cunt. She felt herself dripping and ready. 'Now!'

With a sudden lurch, he pulled her to him and thrust the engorged head of his cock straight into her. The thickness plunged deep, hard, pushing her open. She let out a yell. One of his hands closed over her mouth.

She had the smell of his skin and the warm earth in her nostrils. Pressed up against her inner thighs, the muscular hardness of his body trembled, quivering, poised on the edge of another thrust. She opened her mouth, lips against the rough skin of his palm and let out a moan.

'Yes!' he grunted. His torso twisted, and he thrust forward, thrust deeper into her. She felt her inner muscles loosen. The thickness of him filled her, stretching her, stuffed her full almost to the point of pain. His balls banged against her ass. She raised her hips a fraction and slid on him, groaning into his hand. Hot sweat from his forehead spattered her dress. His forearm pressed hard against her buttocks, pressing her on to him, impaling her.

'Don't stop!' she murmured. He took his hand off her mouth. She said, 'Here!'

Freeing a hand, she pulled at the top of her shift-dress. Stitches tore. He reached behind her, fumbled for the zip, and, in a rush of cool air, her dress slid open. She lay naked to the waist, impaled on his hot cock. He bent his head, sweat visible in his cropped hair, and fastened his lips on her right breast, sucking it into his mouth, teasing it with his tongue, blowing his breath across her suddenly rock-hard nipple.

A spasm rocked her interior flesh. Her hips jammed forward, skin against his skin. She felt his hot body; smelled his arousal strong in her nostrils. The quivers of pre-orgasm raced through her muscles. Still unsatisfied, she moaned, '*Now!*'

Out of control, he threw his strong arms around her, clamping her painfully to his tanned chest. He fell forward, pressing her back. She sprawled down on the bench, lifting her legs. As he thrust, she wrapped her legs around his waist, locking her ankles together behind his taut buttocks. She could not free her arms.

'Oh yes!' he groaned. His body crushed her down. His cock thrust into her, faster now, and faster. Flesh pounded her flesh. She let her head drop back. His hips thumped her hard against the wooden slats of the bench. She strained against him, trying to open wider, to take him all in, all the long, thick, glistening length of his cock—

One of his arms let go. She felt his hand push between them. His fingertips groped down her belly, thrust into her pubic hair and brushed with enticing gentleness across her clit.

Her body exploded with pleasure, her head falling back, banging unnoticed against the bench. Her legs fell, loose, jolting against his body. Again, his finger sought the hard, throbbing nub of her sex.

This time, as arousal seared through her, she felt his hips jerk faster and faster and he spurted, hard, inside her, as she came; all her body convulsing as he filled her, filled her again, filled her to the brim and spilling over, as they slumped down, him on top of her, shudders of pleasure echoing through every part of her body from her shivering scalp to her clenched toes.

'Oh – oh – *wow* . . .'

'Yeah . . .'

Far too soon, he scrambled up and started hauling at his clothes.

'I gotta go!' he said. Hopping, one leg in his jeans, one trying to find the other hole. He jerked his head towards the door.

Outside, she heard the mower's engine – still running.

Chapter Five

AND TWENTY-FOUR HOURS LATER:
'Want a lift back to the house?' Alix asked.

Fern's friend Adam looked up from his sports bag, where he knelt on the gravel attempting to repack it. A warm wind blew across the college car park and ruffled his dark hair. His strong-featured face had an absent-minded expression.

'The house...?'

'Yannis Road? Where you *live*?' A touch of exasperation crept into Alix's tone.

'Oh . . . sure. Thanks.'

As he walked around the front of the car, she leaned across the leather upholstery and opened the passenger door. She stayed stretched out a few seconds longer than necessary, letting him look down at her.

Today, she was wearing a suit: the scarlet skirt hip-hugging and well above the knee, the jacket neatly buttoned together over a sleeveless silk vest. It made her feel like a businesswoman, as well as look like one. As she sat back up in the driver's seat, she felt the strap of her suspender-belt digging into her thigh. She lifted herself a little, wriggling, to adjust it.

'If you, ah, you're sure it's not out of your way?' Adam thumped down into the passenger seat beside her, looking anxiously in her direction. There were probably sports shoes in the bag he'd slung into the back of the car. He was wearing a mud-stained rugby shirt and shorts, and his legs below them were just beginning to tan.

Seeing her look, he said, 'I could change, if you could wait?'

'No, don't worry.' Alix put her hand down and keyed the ignition, sliding her other hand around the gearshift as she manoeuvred it into first gear. The gravel of the car park sprayed out from under the Audi's wheels as she swung the vehicle round. A few drops of rain spattered the windshield as she pulled out into the traffic on the main road.

'What is it you're doing at college, then?' she asked casually, reaching up to tilt the central mirror.

The image in the clear mirror danced, moving out of line for a view of the road behind her. She adjusted it so that she could see Adam's face. To her surprise, his cheeks were pink. She shot a glance at him as she moved up the gears.

'History,' he said. 'Medieval, ah, history.'

'Very intellectual. I see you play sport, though . . .'

One of his thick-fingered hands picked at the mud on his shorts. Short dark hairs grew out of the backs of his fingers, curling and springy, and his nails were short and squared-off. Out of her peripheral vision, she saw him put his hands in his lap and steeple his fingers over his groin. The flush on his face deepened.

'Do you have to get back?' she asked, her lips suddenly dry. She ran her tongue out to moisten them, licking quickly in case he should see. Heavier rain battered the windscreen now. She switched on the wipers. Their rhythmic swish almost drowned out his reply.

'No, I— Not really, no.'

He can't be more than eighteen or nineteen! Alix thought. There was something gangling and coltish about him, despite his short bulk, as if he hadn't yet finished growing into his height or his weight.

Nineteen, and he doesn't know what to make of this . . .
. . . No.
Surely?
He couldn't be. . . ?

'London gets you down, after a while,' she said. 'What about going for a drive in the country? The rain might stop if we get far enough away . . .'

She reached forward to switch on the radio, again leaning more than she needed to. She saw him glance at the buttoned top of her jacket, where it pulled open to show the black silk vest beneath. He turned abruptly away and stared out of the side window.

The rain poured down the windows of the car. She watched him squinting at the world through running streams of water, then quickly turned back to the road. She drove with controlled skill and speed through the back roads, making for the motorway. A turn of her head let her see Adam's breath misting the inside of the cool glass.

Can he *really* be a virgin? The way that Fern was flirting with him—!

But then, she would. And if he's inexperienced, she'd think it was even more fun to wind him up . . .

As Alix turned on to the motorway, the steady thrum of the engine and the background jazz music put her in a mood closer to three a.m. than to four o'clock on an early summer afternoon. A melancholy, pleasurable mood. The traffic was light. She let her foot in her smart black court shoe press down on the accelerator, sending them up past 70 m.p.h. without a second thought.

'Penny for your thoughts?' she said, checking him in the mirror again.

He turned away from the side window, taking his chin off his fist. In the mirror, his eyes met hers. His were pale blue, under heavy dark brows.

'I was just thinking—' His voice squeaked. He coughed. 'Just thinking. We could stop somewhere. Have a drink.'

'Yes, we could.' Alix switched her gaze back to the road. A fine spray kicked up from the road surface. Other vehicles shot past her, lights blazing. Above, through broken clouds, shafts of sunlight poured down into the traffic, making rainbows in the drizzle and spray. She pushed her foot down, breathless with the danger of it.

'Or,' she said, 'we could just stop.'

This time he said nothing. When she glanced momentarily at him, it was to see him frowning. Or was it an expression of pain? Difficult to tell, with those heavy brows and the wide scowling mouth. A rugby bruise on his lip had not fully healed and he rubbed a knuckle over it, staring wordlessly at her.

Alix sighed. 'Okay, forget it.'

'No, I— Wait! Did you mean—?'

His stuttering voice was deep. There was a pleasant trace of an accent in it: he wouldn't be from around London. She reached out to turn the music down.

'Did I mean what?' Alix smiled. She couldn't help the teasing note in her voice.

'When you said "stop", we could – could—' He stuttered to a halt. Spray from a southbound lorry took all her attention for a minute. When he spoke again, over the hum of the engine, he said, 'We could – get to know each other better.'

'But do you want to?'

He sounded puzzled. 'Want to?'

'What else do we need to know?' Alix said. 'I want you. You want me. You've been hiding a hard-on for the last thirty miles—'

He spluttered. She spoke over it:

'—I fancy you, or I wouldn't have invited you into my car and told you, now would I? So why bother with all that let's-have-a-drink, let's-pretend-we-care-about-each-other's-opinions stuff? Do you want to fuck? Do you want to fuck *me*?'

Just hearing herself say it aloud, to a man, was a turn-on. She felt herself creaming her pants. A warmth stole over her skin, from her thighs to her breasts and crept up to blush in her cheeks. She shot him a fast glance.

'Well?'

'*Yes*!'

'Well, then . . .' Alix noted the road sign, and flicked her indicator. She pulled off into the slip lane, slowing, and took the Audi carefully round a sharp bend at the top of the exit road. 'Let's find somewhere to pull over.'

'But . . .' Adam's voice sounded agonised. His hands in his lap knotted into fists. He said, 'You've done this before.'

'Not quite *this*. I don't make a habit of abducting men and fucking them – though I can't think why not!' Alix grinned to herself. 'In fact, I've only had one encounter in the last few months.'

But what an encounter that was! – Adam, you've got a way to go to beat Tom . . .

She added, 'So you needn't sit there thinking I'm a slut. I just don't see why *I* shouldn't do the asking, for once. You'd be surprised how much fun it is!'

While she was talking, she scanned the road signs, driving off into leafy lanes. The Audi began to climb up from the bottom of a steep hill. She shifted down the gears.

'And anyway,' Alix said suddenly, 'I'm cheating a bit, because I *know* you fancy me – Fern told me.'

'*Fern!*' The name came out sounding like a swear word. Adam scowled. 'She put you up to this? But you're not like her friends ... I thought you'd be too mature for that sort of rubbish.'

The light dimmed, the rain coming down harder now. The Audi went under trees. She flicked on the headlights and slowed her speed. As they came out from under the trees again and crested the hill, she swung the wheel over abruptly. The Audi glided to a halt in a beauty-spot parking space: an area of gravel overlooking the sharp drop-off of the land. Rain and cloud swept up, blocking the long view.

Alix reached out and turned the engine off. Silence, apart from the noise of the rain. She swivelled around in her seat, the leather creaking, so that she could sit sideways and look at him properly.

'Adam, Fern didn't "put me up" to anything. She said you fancied me. This was a few weeks back, just after I came to the college. Now if she's wrong, just tell me, and we'll drive back to London and no harm done.'

He sat forward in the car seat, head down, hands hanging between his knees. He didn't look at her. She wanted to reach out and ruffle his crisp dark hair, but she forced herself not to move. Just looking at the strength of his shoulders and the muscled tautness of his hips made her breath come short in her throat.

'I do fancy you,' Adam said. He still didn't look at her. 'Fern's a cow. I didn't know she was going to tell you I said it. I didn't know you'd ... I won't be any good to you,' he said in a rush, staring at the floor of the car. 'I ... haven't done this before, you see.'

I was right, she thought, dazed. *I wanted to initiate a younger man. All that strength, all that firm body – and no one's had it yet ... I could be his first. If that's what he wants ...*

Gently she said, 'I don't want to be anyone's girlfriend, Adam. I just want us to enjoy each other. If you'd rather wait until you're with someone who does want something permanent – that's fine.'

'No, I'd rather this!' he blurted, sitting up and looking her in the face. His expression was unguarded and open. 'I don't want to mess it up when I'm with someone I care about – oh shit! I didn't mean that the way it sounded. I mean, if it's a girlfriend, and I ruin it because it's my first time – I mean, it matters if I ruin it with you, but – no, not "but", that's not what I mean—'

'*Adam.*' She gave way to her desire, and reached out to put her fingertips against his lips. They were wonderfully soft, contrasting with his masculine body. Under her fingers, she felt his hot breath and the quiver of his mouth.

'Adam, everybody's got to have a first time. There's no need to be scared.' She took her fingers away.

'I *do* fancy you,' he repeated, looking miserable. 'But you're not like the rest of them – they're girls, and you're a woman. They don't know any more than I do, most of them. But you . ... I don't want to be laughed at.'

Alix dropped her hand into his lap. She slid her hand palm down under his hands, into his crotch. The huge thickness of his cock sprang into her palm, hot even through the material of his shorts.

'Nobody's going to laugh at *that*,' she said softly.

'But . . .'

'No,' she said, reaching with her other hand to turn the music back on, 'no, you stop worrying. Just let me show you . . .'

Carefully, she put out one hand. She touched a fingertip to his bruised mouth, tracing the line of his lip. His skin shivered under her touch. She felt a tautness in her stomach; a craving for physical satisfaction – *no*, she thought: *hunger. Plain hunger*.

He watched her, saying nothing as she slid her fingers around to cup his cheek. He was not far from the gangling, unfinished state of adolescence. But her thumb caressed the fine shaved stubble on his chin. Suddenly she clenched her hand in his crisp dark curls, holding his hair at the back of his neck, and brought his head forward. She fastened her lips on his, kissing, licking, thrusting her tongue in to meet his and twine with it.

For a split second he didn't react. Then she felt the heat of his mouth, the aliveness of his body, as both of his hands came up behind her head and pressed her towards him. His warm, soft lips moved under hers, nibbling at her full lower lip.

Abruptly he let go; sat back. 'I don't know if I—'

'*What?*' Half dizzy, half shaken, Alix slumped back into the driver's seat. Her body hummed like a struck glass. Wanting him vibrated through her, through her shaking hands and her tense belly. *He's tough and strong and he's untouched—*

'I don't know what I'm doing!' he groaned.

Breathless, Alix managed to get out, 'Are you doing what you want?'

'Yes!' His dark blue eyes fixed on hers, under the thunderous brows. She saw that his eyelashes were long and dark and soft, strangely contrasting with his heavy masculine nose and chin. 'This is what I want . . . more than anything.'

'Then don't you do a thing . . .'

The rain beat harder on the car window now. Water

flooded down in grey streams. The outside world was invisible. A faint condensation misted the glass, and the jazz playing from the radio seemed suddenly a long way away. She felt a rush of pure adrenalin, spearing her under the breastbone. *I am going to touch him. I am going to make him come.*

'Give me your hand . . . I'll show you something you can do.'

As he reached out, hesitantly, she took his strong hand. His fingers were hot. Keeping her eyes on his face, she moved one foot closer to her, bending her knee. His pupils dilated in the rain-dark interior of the car.

She kept hold of his hand, and thrust it under the hem of the tight scarlet skirt. Momentarily, she brushed his fingertips against her thigh, above the top of her stocking. Then she pushed his hand further in, further up her skirt. His fingers touched the silk panties at her crotch. She felt him flinch back, for a second, and then his hand and wrist moved out of her grip, and she felt him cup her mound of Venus. He gasped, his eyes shining with wonder. His warm palm pressed down on her.

'You may not have done this before,' she said, half gasping, 'but you've got all the right instincts— Ah! Ah, yes . . .'

Alix shut her eyes. She felt his thick thumb pressing down on her mound, on the sweat-slicked pussy hair, and his fingers pressing up against the crotch of her panties. The slick material was sodden with hot juices. She couldn't help moving on his hand. She slid herself gently back and forwards, looking at the world through half-closed lashes.

'Oh yes . . . oh, *yes* . . .'

There was a sudden coldness, an absence of his hand

against her flesh. She opened her eyes. He sat staring at her, a straining erection tenting the front of his shorts.

'I don't—' He swallowed. 'I don't want you to – to enjoy yourself too soon . . .'

'What? *Oh*.' She grinned, feeling her lips skin back from her teeth. 'It isn't like that for girls. I can come as often as I like. But I think we ought to do something about *that* . . .'

As she spoke, she leaned forward, letting him have a good look down her jacket that was still buttoned up tight. She let one hand drift into his lap again, barely brushing the skin of her palm over his crotch. The heat of his cock came through the thin material. She saw him grimace as the throbbing hard-on strained after her touch.

'Well, *I* can't!' he exclaimed. 'I don't want to come too soon – oh, shit!'

With a deep-voiced curse, he moved forward on the car seat. One of his arms came around her shoulders, keeping her bent across the gearstick and central part of the car, and pinning her arms to her side. He plunged his other hand down the front of her jacket, wrenching off its buttons as his hot fist worked down under her silk vest, under her bra cup, to grab a handful of her breast. Her nipple instantly hardened in his palm.

'Oh, my God—'

Alix felt herself sprawling forward, her bum, tightly encased in her skirt, jutting into the air. She landed half in his lap.

Without trying to move her arms, she nuzzled her face into his belly, nipping the waistband of his shorts between her neat white teeth. She pulled, tugged, trying to shift them down his body.

He swore under his breath. She felt him brace leg and hip against parts of the car. She couldn't help but giggle, even with her mouth full of cloth. As he shifted his body up, she turned her head, and with his help pulled the shorts down. The red, shiny, engorged cock sprang loose of the cloth, veins tightly outlined on the swelling flesh.

She dipped her head, before he could say a word, and closed her lips over the head. It quivered in her mouth, heating, swelling even more. She heard him gasp above her. She wanted him to put a hand down her pants, but there was no way to tell him, no time, as he groaned and arched his back—

Before she could do more than slide the tip of her tongue around his glans, he came in her mouth. Copiously, flooding; thrusting his hips up, so that she buried her face in the warm, slick, soft flesh of his belly, while she sucked him dry.

'Oh, shit, sorry – *sorry*—'

She leaned back into his lap, cleaning herself delicately, and grinned up at him.

'It'll last longer next time,' she said. 'And next time won't be long – you'll be surprised . . .'

'But—'

She lay on her back, looking up at him. With one hand, she undid the surviving buttons of her jacket, pulling up her silk vest to expose her belly and the bottom of her bra. The same hand crept down to her side, unzipping her skirt.

'You've got fingers and a tongue,' she said. 'While you're waiting, I'll show you what to do. First, I want you to suck my nipples. Then you put your fingers down my knickers and right up me—'

She broke off with a gasp. His strong, stiff-fingered

hand jabbed down into her clothes. She lifted her hips, tilting her pelvic girdle. His hot, thick fingers plunged into the heat of her cunt, sliding in the wetness, groping for direction. She freed a hand to grasp his wrist and steady him.

'There – ohhh!'

The solid stiffness of him slid into her, pressing her inner lips apart. Her flesh sang, straining against him; her clitoris stiffening, her inner walls swelling and flowering open.

'Move!' she growled, but it wasn't necessary. As if her body told his, without words, he began to shove his hand up and in, hard as a piston. Her body loosened, tensed – *no need for foreplay!* she realised, amazed – and he thrust, thrust, thrust; hard and fast, hard and fast—

Friction became fire: as he drove his fingers into her, she came, cunt convulsing, clitoris throbbing; came with a suddenness and hardness that made her soar up to the peaks of sensation and drop down, heated skin thrilling with cold shivers; and soar again, again: with the piercing pleasure of that orgasmic fire.

Panting and lying limply across his lap, she looked up into his face. He smiled at her with a wonderful gentleness; a look of wonder, wanting and absurd pride.

'Well, look at you . . . Maybe I'm going to be okay at this. Do you think? I could do it again now, I reckon,' Adam said. 'What about you?'

Voice still breaking and her whole body throbbing, Alix said, 'Oh – I suppose I could force myself . . .'

—and I am sorry not to have written them down for you before I did them! I hope this won't spoil the scientific methodology of the project.

Alix paused, looking at the brief lines she had

written to Professor Mayhew. She smiled reminiscently. After a moment, she added:

And I'll come in for the first interview/debrief on Wednesday, as we arranged.

Chapter Six

'Way cool ... But it's very evident that you're not stretching yourself,' a male voice said.

The voice came from behind Alix. She started, trying to swing around in Professor Mayhew's saggy armchair and see who else had come into the office.

Sandro Elliot stood leaning against the door frame. He had evidently been reading the monitor screen over Vivienne Mayhew's shoulder. Alix blushed.

' "Stretching herself?" ' Professor Mayhew queried. Her voice trailed off into a delicious gurgle and something that in a woman twenty years younger might have been a snigger. 'Sandro, if you've nothing better to contribute to this—'

'What do you *mean*, not stretching myself?' Alix queried. She felt her cheeks heat and turned away. She wouldn't look at the tall American.

I didn't know he knew about the Professor's project ... oh shit!

Wanting him's bad enough, she thought, but wanting him while he's laughing at me – that's a *bitch*.

'Well, look at it,' the American voice said from behind her. 'Not very exciting fantasies, are they? A Lady Chatterley bonk with the gardener, who won't follow up in case he loses his job. And the seduction of a male virgin . . .'

Something about Elliot's tone caught her attention. Alix thought, *you're not as indifferent as you sound*. She swung around, resting her arm on the back of the armchair, and gazed up at him. Today, in summer sandals and sundress, she felt she could be as young as the students who doubtless drooled over him in lectures. She gave him a shaky flirty grin.

'So what *would* be exciting?' she demanded.

Sandro Elliot turned away from her, speaking only to Vivienne Mayhew. 'It's the trouble with all of your students on this project. Vanilla sex.'

'That's a dangerous world out there,' Professor Mayhew said mildly. 'Don't forget, these are women who have a conviction of the importance of their own sexual needs, such that it drives them to fulfil them in the real world. That alone makes it far from "vanilla". If she were one of the control group, now—'

Puzzled, Alix put in, 'Control group?'

'Oh – yes. We have a set of secure rooms here,' Vivienne Mayhew said. She crossed her stockinged legs neatly at the ankle, swinging back and forth a little on her office chair. Alix had a brief mental image of thin ropes crossing those ankles, binding the older brunette to the chair; ropes that would tie her hands behind her and cross her body, digging into the cotton print dress that covered her lush breasts—

'. . . A set of rooms in which I can run the control group,' Professor Mayhew was saying. 'Those are a group of female students who masturbate to fantasies and then write down what sort of fantasies excite them most. In that way I hope to see whether the women who are putting their fantasies into practice are, as Sandro suggests, only living out the vanilla version.'

Alix turned from her to Sandro Elliot, to see what the tall man's reaction might be. She found herself looking past Elliot's rangy torso into the amazed face of Professor Jordan Axley.

'You have a *what*?' the dark-haired man squeaked from the corridor outside Professor Mayhew's office. 'They're not just writing this, they're – *doing it*?'

Despite the heat of early June, Professor Jordan Axley still wore a charcoal pinstripe suit. His shoes were brilliantly polished, Alix noted, and his tie knotted with extreme care. Above this perfection, the sight and sound of his outrage sent her off into a peal of giggles. She clapped her hands over her mouth.

'Why, yes, Jordan.' Vivienne Mayhew's gaze was mischievously demure. 'I'm thinking of setting up a male control group, in fact, to discover how men's ideas about women's fantasies match the reality – or don't. They could see if their masturbatory fantasies are the same as the women's. Would you like me to put you down for a place on it? Or perhaps a place on the "experimental" side? I had considered doing a complementary study with males . . .'

Like this, but for men? Alix thought. Simultaneously, she found herself staring into Sandro Elliot's face and turning bright red. A little smile played about his mouth. He rubbed his hand across his jaw and the rasp of skin on blond stubble drove her crazy. She felt herself melting, creaming her pants. *If he could be part of this experiment—*

'How about it?' she said huskily. 'I've still got some fantasies to put into action, Mr Elliot. I promise you, they aren't "vanilla". How about . . .'

Sandro Elliot's strong-featured face took on a strange expression. For a moment, she would have sworn he looked panicky. The tall American turned away from her, looking down at Vivienne Mayhew.

'I could, like, join your male control group, maybe?' he said.

The brunette frowned slightly. 'You realise the groups can't interact? It would spoil the results.'

He shrugged lanky shoulders. 'Sure. No problem.' And turning his dark, North-Sea-blue eyes back to Alix, he repeated, 'No problem.'

Jordan Axley snickered. 'Too bad, Miss...? Miss. Real men don't, as you'll find, appreciate come-ons from every little tramp—'

Vivienne's voice cut sharply across his: *'Professor Axley.'*

The dark-haired man flushed, colour rising up his neck, his forehead going bright pink.

'Professor Axley,' she repeated, 'you have a very ... strange ... idea of female sexuality. A woman who looks after her own sexual needs is not a tramp. A woman who takes the initiative in sex is doing the most healthy thing she can do – tending to her own needs and desires. That is *not* something you should criticise.'

Oh shit, that's done it ...

Alix, shifting in the armchair to interrupt, realised it was too late. The dark-haired man's blush changed from pink to dull red. He scowled.

That wasn't the tone to take with him, Alix thought. Professor Mayhew, you may be good on sexuality, but you don't know when you're pissing a guy off ...

'I,' Jordan Axley said, with a magisterial manner that would have sounded pompous coming from a man twice his age, '*I* consider this whole project utterly repugnant. I cannot believe the college is prepared to fund filth like this! And perhaps, Professor Mayhew, you'll find that they won't be – when they know exactly what's going on here!'

He was plainly looking for a door to slam, but being out in the corridor cramped his style, Alix thought. He settled for glaring at each one of them, turning on his heel and stomping off towards the door to the stairwell.

'Jordan!' Vivienne Mayhew called. 'Jordan – oh, *damn*.'

'Is he going to be a problem?' Sandro Elliot mused, in a low masculine purr that made Alix's skin shiver.

'The college authorities *do* know what I'm doing. I'm not stupid.' Vivienne's gypsy-olive brow furrowed. 'I don't need an enemy, though. He won't be able to do anything overt . . . but I wouldn't put covert sabotage past him. Damn, I shouldn't have upset him. He's always hair-trigger where sex is concerned.'

Alix whooped.

'What?' Vivienne said. 'What? *Oh*. No, I didn't mean – well, for all I know he may be – but—'

Her voice shook, and she caught Alix's eye. Alix felt the breath tight in her chest. She struggled for air, couldn't get it past the giggles and whoops of laughter that the glance provoked. She sprawled back in the armchair, dress riding up to bare half her thighs. Catching Sandro's expression as the American academic looked down, she found her amusement vanishing.

He turned me down. He couldn't make it plainer. What *is* it with him!

'Put my name down, Vivienne,' the tall American said, shifting himself off the door frame with a shove of his shoulders. 'Your control group, don't forget.'

Open-mouthed, Alix stared at the empty door after he left.

'There is one interesting thing in your report,' Professor Mayhew said musingly. 'This first man, the gardener, Tom. Tall and fair-haired, you say. Doesn't that sound a little like someone else we know?'

Alix stood, smoothing down her summer dress. A light film of sweat dampened her torso, and the cool breeze from the open office window was welcome.

'Okay, I fancy the pants off Sandro!' she confessed. 'But if I was thinking of him when I was with Tom, I certainly don't remember it.'

'Possibly a subconscious impulse...' Vivienne Mayhew made a brief note on the file in front of her.

'And Adam's nothing like him.'

'The exact opposite, in fact – an untried boy. Were you trying to make him jealous, perhaps?'

'My life doesn't revolve around Mr Sandro Elliot!' Alix snapped. 'Why would it? He obviously wouldn't have me if I was the last thing with tits and a cunt alive on the face of the earth! And as for vanilla – I'll show him *vanilla*!'

'Alix,' the older woman said warningly, 'be careful. Seeing to your own needs doesn't mean abandoning common sense.'

Alix nodded absently. 'Sure ... but you wait until you read my next report. You wait until *he* reads it. I'll make him wish he wasn't on the "theoretical" side of this experiment!'

'No, that's okay,' Alix said. She kept the cellphone close to her mouth, and her voice low, just in case anyone should overhear her. 'Just meet me at the station, first. You know where they do this? And they *do* still do it? Good. See you there, Jack. 'Bye.'

She crossed the street and walked into the entrance of the Underground station, then went down the escalator. The platform was not crowded. Hot air drifted along, pushed by the distant trains in other tunnels of the system. Alix could all but taste the spark of electricity from the rails, carried in the stale breeze. She kept alert for the push of air that would mean her train was coming.

Good old Jack. Maybe I shouldn't have given him the push last year ... but we don't have anything in common, really. And his idea of great sex *was* pretty much wham-bang-how-was-it-for-you ...

She trod with care along the platform, passing the posters advertising tourist attractions and art shows. The high stiletto heels she was wearing took practice to balance in. *And even if they are classic Italian-leather evening shoes,* she thought, *and the sort of bargain you dream about – that still doesn't mean they're exactly* comfortable.

The lights on the board flicked over, counting down. People – mostly tourists with cameras and wearing the lightest summer clothes – drifted towards the edge of the platform. Alix felt the hot, stale air on her face and moved out to meet the train.

Her skin felt as though it was running with sweat under the light summer coat she wore. *If I had the nerve to show how I'm dressed, I wouldn't be this uncomfortable ...* She tugged the tie-belt a little more firmly around her at the thought. Her heels tap-tapped as she stepped up into the carriage. The doors hissed closed behind her.

She studied her own reflection in the curving glass quite deliberately. The heels made her taller. Against the blackness outside, her hair shone silver, drawn up into a French plait. The sapphires at her ear lobes sparked similar blue fire from her eyes. And the tie-belt of the plain ivory summer coat snugged in around her waist, accentuating the curves of breasts and hips, but hiding whatever might be beneath. And given that the coat came barely halfway down her thighs ...

This is mad! she thought. She met the eyes of the woman in the glass again, looking for some sign of recklessness, or courage. There was only a tight, worried expression to be seen.

You've got a cellphone with emergency numbers on. You're going to give a false name. Jack will know what's happened to you. There's nothing to be worried about.

Oh, but there is, she answered her internal voice, swaying with the rocking of the train. At each station, she saw fewer tourists, more Londoners; and the platforms were getting shabbier each time. *Oh, there is. Because, if this works, Jack won't know where I've gone, or who I'm with. And if I lose the phone – if it gets taken away from me . . . well. Because, if this works, I won't have any control over what happens to me tonight.*

A pulse of arousal swept through her. She felt moisture start out on her bare shoulders, under the light coat. A trickle of sweat ran down her collarbone, and between her breasts.

This *is* dangerous. And it *is* crazy.

And it *is* what I want to do.

By the time they crossed the river and went through more stations, she had her confidence back. She didn't sit down, even though there were seats. She preferred to sway a little, holding the upright steel bar, as if the train rocked to a music of which only she could hear the rhythm.

The train hissed to a halt. Before her eyes, the name of the station came into focus, and she hurriedly tap-tapped across the carriage and down on to the platform. This one was all but deserted. She gazed around at the white and green tiles and the blowing litter. Behind her, the Tube train's doors hissed shut. A whirl of wind blew about her ankles as it pulled out of the station.

'Hey, Alix,' a familiar voice said behind her.

She turned, smiling, and looked up at the man waiting for her. 'Jack. Am I glad to see you. This place has got scary.'

'Nah, you've just gone upmarket.' He hunched his fists into the pockets of his donkey jacket, which she saw he still wore despite it being summer. The knees of his jeans were out, and spatters of paint marked the cloth. He grinned at her, lines crinkling around his bloodshot blue eyes. His hair was shaven down to a fuzz, so close that he appeared to be bald. That and his thick neck and hulking shoulders gave him a skinhead look.

'There is a game on tonight?' she asked, double-checking.

If he says 'yes', I'm going through with this. If he says 'no' – well, that wouldn't be so bad; I don't think he'd mind a night together for old time's sake. I'd forgotten quite how dishy a bit of rough trade he is...

'Come on.' He jerked his head. As he started to walk, she saw that he was wearing cement-stained trainers, all but falling to bits. *Come straight off the site*, she thought.

'They going to let you into the game looking like that?' She hastened, on tiptoe, to keep up with his stride. He moved easily up the Tube station steps, leaving her panting in his wake. 'Damn it, Jack!'

He turned and waited for her at the top of the steps, one bitten-nailed hand on the steps. He grinned. He pulled his jacket open, and she saw the top of a thick bundle of notes in his inside pocket. 'Yeah, I'm in the game.'

'I'll pay you back,' she said hastily, 'like we arranged. I don't expect you to do this for me at your own expense.'

'I ain't asked you for anything,' he said. As she made the top of the steps, he reached out and put his arm around her waist. She felt herself pulled towards him, pressed against his work clothes, and the solid bulk of his body. He felt warm, sexy, comforting and, above all, safe.

Too safe.

'Could do, but I won't,' he added, bent his shaved head unselfconsciously, and kissed her very lightly on the lips. His own lips were soft and hot. She felt his breath feather her cheek. 'But we were never nothing to each other, babe. Except for the fucking. That was good. This is nothing, this cash; I can make twice as much in a week.'

He might be boasting, she thought, or he might well be telling the truth. She linked her arm through his, her tiny bag clamped under her other arm. As they walked towards the escalator, she said, 'Okay . . . where are we going?'

'Try the Marquis of Granby first.'

She saw him grinning, standing beside her on the moving escalator. The machinery carried her upwards, on towards the outside world. Seemingly unstoppable. *But there's another escalator the other side, when we get to the top. I could just turn around and go straight back home again.*

'And for Chrissakes remember you're my girlfriend for the evening, will you? You got a face on you like you're sucking a lemon.'

As he spoke, his arm left her waist and drifted down. She felt the flat of his palm against her buttock, under the material of her summer coat. Arousal pulsed in her clit. She pushed back a little against him.

'Ah, that's my girl!'

And, of course, the other reason I dumped you is that you're as sensitive as a brick . . .

The moving steel platforms carried her onward. She felt the pressure of his hand cupped around her bum. Knowing it wouldn't take much to let him slide his hand under the cloth, push his thick stubby fingers between her thighs . . . She swallowed, dry-mouthed, wanting to fuck him here and now, right here—

'The Marquis is up this way. Better hurry. Don't want all the places taken, do we?'

The light outside both glared and threw dim shadows. She barely registered the broken pavement, automatically keeping her balance in the high heels. Old kebab wrappers blew along the street. The cars parked at the side of the road were either old bangers or brand new and very expensive indeed. The orange street lights blotted out the last of the summer sky, sunset still visible at ten in the evening.

On the next corner, people were standing outside the pub in the street. The crowd had spilled out, glasses in hands, and the people were standing in groups, talking in loud voices. One or two of the men stared at her as Jack pushed his way through towards the saloon-bar door. She found herself automatically closing the distance between herself and him, and was annoyed. *How do I think I'm going to go through with this if I can't even walk into a pub on my own!*

She followed his broad back through the doors. Inside, it was impossibly crowded. Elbows and shoulders pushed against her, and she twisted neatly to avoid having beer spilled on her ivory-coloured coat. Someone said cheerfully, 'Mind out, darlin'!' Jack forged ahead, not stopping near the packed bar. She saw at last that he was heading for one of the doors at the back. He exchanged a brief word with a man sitting at a table next to the door – the voices and laughter were too loud for her to hear what either of them said.

Finally, Jack pulled open his donkey jacket. The man nodded and reached out, pushing the door open a fraction. Jack went through it without one look behind to see if she followed. She caught the door before it swung to, and went through.

Smoke greyed-out the air, and the smaller room stank of stale beer, despite the fact that all the sash windows were open to the London night. Six or seven men sat around at table, and another two or three on the benches against the wall. Those at the table were dressed in expensive suits, and there were gold signet rings on most hands. The faces shared nothing but an intent immobility, even as they studied their cards.

'You get yourself a drink, babe,' Jack said. He winked at her. 'And you can take that off in here, fuck knows it's hot enough.'

His hand slid down from her shoulder to her waist, and tugged at her tie-belt. She shrugged his hand away. She did not smile. With an expressionless face, she undid the belt and slid the coat off her shoulders, trailing it from her hand for a moment.

The atmosphere in the room changed.

What she wore was conservative, almost – a short party dress that came halfway down her stockinged thighs. It was cut discreetly across the bust, barely showing the cleft of her cleavage, and held up by two spaghetti-straps made of fine black metal links. It curved in to her waist, clung to her hips, and then stopped, leaving uncovered the long firm expanse of her thighs.

What made them look, she knew, was that it was oyster silk under fine black lace, and for a second – just a second – it looked as though she might be naked under a see-through black lace dress.

The mixture of class and tart turned heads. She

gazed back at them with ice-grey eyes.

'A drink, darlin'!' Jack slapped her lightly on her bottom. 'Get one for me too, will yer?'

Without particularly hurrying, she catwalked over towards the small private bar. She kept her back to the assembled men and the poker game. Behind her, their voices started up again: short grunts, low bids, a half-choked-off exclamation over bad luck.

She put her coat and bag carefully down on one of the bar stools, ordered wine and sat herself neatly on the next bar stool. The wine was sour, and aromatic, and dizzying; and she settled for cradling her drink in her hands and looking across the room with an expression of utter boredom.

A girlfriend who giggled and talked would have faded into the background. Alix felt butterflies in her stomach. It's working, she thought. Look unattainable, look like an ice-maiden ... and they want what they can't have.

Glances turned her way as the evening went on. The sky outside changed to black. She sipped at the wine. Her stomach churned too much for her to think about eating and the wine on an empty stomach might make her sick, so she drank very little. Her gaze wandered around the room, from time to time settling on one of the card-players. Jack. A big blond man in an Armani suit. An older man with slicked-back black hair. A fatter man, four or five years younger than her, with glasses and a wide-eyed innocent expression. Another older man, ten or fifteen years her senior, with crisp white curls and the odour of expensive aftershave. Another ...

Which one?

She almost missed it when it started. Jack's voice rose in half-drunk anger.

'I can bet what I fucking well like! She'll do what I say. She's class, she is. She's worth *double* this piddling amount of money!'

Alix kept her voice steady with an effort. She heard herself even manage to sound bored as she spoke across the suddenly quiet room. 'Jack, what are you doing now? Have you lost all your money again?'

'Mouthy bitch.' He scowled. 'You keep your mouth shut. I got no more money, but I've got you. And you're on the table now.' He gestured at the crumpled notes on the tabletop and the cards and sniggered. 'I'm putting a night with you into the pot. Come on now, gentlemen. You only got to look at her. Don't let that po-face fool you. She's a right little goer once you get her behind closed doors.'

Oh thanks, Jack! Alix thought. She caught the amusement in his eye. *Good old Jack, anything for a laugh. I knew you'd do this well. But if it goes wrong . . . how much help are you going to be?*

The Italian-looking middle-aged man said, 'No, we don't do this—'

'Aw, come on, Nico! I got no more money—'

The man with white curls, in a slightly Germanic accent – or Dutch, maybe – said, 'Why not? The lady makes no objection. Perhaps she hires by the hour anyway.'

Oh God, if they think I'm a prostitute, they'll . . .

Something between fear and a delicious curdle of arousal ran through her entire body. The small back room of a pub, in the real world; not a fantasy, not something that would vanish when she opened her eyes.

'Mmm? Yeah.' The one called Nico nodded. 'Perhaps. Chris? Daniel? Mr Baxani?'

The young fat boy in the spectacles nodded, as did

the big man in the Armani suit, and a Hindu man who had been sitting so quietly among them that she hadn't noticed him.

'Then we play,' the Dutchman said.

He looked at Jack with such contempt that Alix was surprised Jack didn't notice. *And he doesn't – he's not that good an actor.* She saw him through the Dutchman's eyes: a thuggish Englishman fresh off the building site, with a roll of black-market money and a high-priced prostitute, and without the sense not to be fleeced of both.

What have I got myself into?

The normal world lay just the other side of the room's door. She heard the babble of voices in the bar, and in the street outside. It wouldn't take much to cross back into it now – a few steps. They might swear at her, or at Jack, but it wouldn't be serious; she could expect to walk away from it. *But if I let this go further—*

The fat boy made a soft-voiced bid. The Armani suit requested cards. As he reached forward, she admired the strength of his shoulders and the length of his arm. Nothing showed on his face as he took the cards into his hand. Another bid: from the Italian-looking Nico, forty-five if he was a day. And the Hindu, Baxani: sharp-faced and elegant, and a little darker-skinned than Lewis Kumar at the office.

Alix shut her eyes. She swayed slightly on the stool, but kept her balance. She became intensely conscious of her body, of her oyster-silk dress clinging to her breasts and waist and hips, and the heavier black lace that pressed the silk into every curve and dip of her body. The minuscule metal straps bit into her bare shoulders, and with her hair clipped up, the back of her neck felt naked and unprotected.

She hooked her heels into the rung of the stool and

shifted her bottom on the hard wooden seat. Sweat and heat burned between her thighs. She felt herself damp and hot, juices trickling down over her swelling labia. *I am being put up as a stake in a card game and I have no control over who wins me.*

Or what they do to me then.

'Mine,' a voice said.

She opened her eyes to find the table of men staring at her. For a second she couldn't work out who had spoken. Then a flat-fingered hand, with springy black hairs growing out of the backs of the fingers, came down proprietorially on the cards. The middle-aged, sweaty, black-haired man: Nico.

Jack whined, 'Nico, you know I was only joking—'

'I never joke about cards.' The middle-aged man stood up. He was short, Alix saw; shorter than she was in these heels. He looked behind him and nodded. One of the men sitting there went to the window, the other to the door; the one at the door spoke quietly to the man outside.

The third man who had been sitting there came and leaned on the back of Jack's chair. He had a calm face, and a smart dark suit, and you would not have picked him out of a line-up, so unremarkable did he appear.

'I don't joke,' Nico repeated.

Oh shit! Alix thought. I didn't know Jack knew anybody this dodgy. Oh shit: don't let him be into drugs – I'm going home. I'm going home *now*.

She got down from the bar stool, stumbling slightly, and grabbed her bag and coat in one hand. When she looked up from finding her footing, another of the men in dark suits was standing in front of her – and far too close to her. She looked up at him. The suit was well cut, but the man in it had a wrestler's body.

She looked helplessly across at Jack, her eyes filled

with panic. He quickly shook his head.

No one spoke to her. The man held her by the upper arm, and moved her forward at just slightly faster than walking pace. She found herself in a tight group of men: Nico and his followers. Moving through the door, through another door and out of the crowded bar; staggering in a suddenly cold back alley, and then bundled with one hand on her head as the man ducked her into the back of a limousine.

The engine kicked smoothly into life. Before she had a chance to open the door and get out again, they were moving. Not fast, but too fast to throw herself out without some injury. She swivelled round in the seat and found herself facing the man called Nico.

'Look . . .' Her voice dried in her throat.

You don't argue with a man like this. Oh God, just let me get out of this safely—

'You don't understand,' she finished weakly.

He sat looking forward, past the driver's head, and not at her. His skin was sallow and his hair was so blue-black that she was certain it was dyed. Short, stout and with a belly that pushed out over the belt of his expensive suit . . .

And from his dyed hair to his polished shoes, he's a man who can do what he likes with me. Whether *I* like it or not. And I certainly wouldn't have chosen *him*.

'Jack isn't my boyfriend,' she said, feeling as if she were arguing in *Alice in Wonderland*. 'I'm not his to bet!'

He reached out a hand, without even looking at her, and pushed his palm into her mouth. She felt herself pushed back hard against the headrest of the seat – under the deceptive flab, there must have been real strength. He leaned forward and said something to the driver, still pinning her.

Speechless, she brought her hands up and grabbed

at his wrist with one and pried at his fingers with the other. He took his hand away. Before she had time to do more than gasp in relief, he shifted around in his seat, took hold of her shoulders, and looked into her face. He had been eating rich food; it was on his breath. She smelled his warm sweaty body.

She couldn't help it: she squirmed where she sat. His power over her made her muscles go weak and her cleft heat up. She became aware she was breathing fast, her breasts rising and falling under the silk and lace. She imagined him putting his hand down the front of her dress as his next step. Her nipples hardened just at the thought.

'Ah.' He sounded satisfied, but puzzled. Still holding her by her shoulders, he put her back at arm's length, looking her up and down. 'You're not a prostitute. What are you doing here? What is that boy to you? Who sent you?'

'Nobody *sent* me.' A split second later, she realised that only the genuine incredulity in her tone could have convinced him she was speaking the truth. She blushed, feeling her cheeks heat up. Still holding eye contact with him – and he had deep brown, wonderfully lashed eyes – she said, 'I asked Jack to do it for me. I wanted to know what it would be like.'

He stared at her. After a moment, he chuckled; a deep, rich, well-fed sound. He shook his head. She held her breath, not knowing quite what amused him.

'So you did,' he said at last. 'So you did. And you got me. And I got you. My winnings.'

Something in his tone made her squirm again, as if the leather seat pressing up into her crotch could exert enough pressure to give her relief. Something possessive in his tone made her shiver.

'You expect me to stop the car?' he said, curiously.

'And let you out? Of course you do. This is not an area of London I should care to walk alone at night in. Where do you live? I will take you there. Or drop you off nearby.'

'You—'

There was nothing in his expression but honesty. Some feeling of unreality that had been growing in her in the pub, aided by the wine, suddenly collapsed. She found herself cold and sober – stone-cold sober. *This is the real world. I could have this offer, or I could end up behind a dustbin in some alley. Just thank God he's a sensible man, even if he is a criminal.*

'That's very kind of you,' she said, her breathing easier.

She stared at him for a moment. London's dark streets glided by outside.

'We could go to your place,' she said in a rush.

'What?'

'I can walk home in the morning,' Alix said. 'You *did* win me. If you want to . . . we could carry on with that.'

For a moment, she surprised an expression of vulnerability on to his face; gone before she properly realised it was there. Then he smiled, once.

'Yes. I did win you. You would be mine, I suppose. To do *exactly* as I like with.'

Taking no notice of the driver of the car hardly a yard away, the Italian-looking man reached forward and put his hand up her dress. She felt his thick fingers at her thighs, rubbing the material of her stockings. Quickly, his hand pushed further in, to where the naked tops of her thighs were cool and sweaty. His probing fingers reached her crotch, thrust in—

'Ah, you are wet,' he said. 'That is a bad girl. You should be punished.'

Arousal left her speechless. She opened her lips, and

could only gasp. *This is stupid: I've no guarantee he'll let me go home in the morning – I don't even know where he's taking me—!*

The car stopped.

The headlights went off. Dazzling light replaced by sudden darkness: she could only respond to the tug on her arm as he took his hand out of her panties and pulled her out of the car. She stumbled on a kerb. Something dark loomed all around – buildings? Confused, she could only stagger, propelled in front of him by his surprisingly strong grip, trying desperately to keep her balance in the stiletto heels.

Not until she found herself in a metal lift, rising, did she realise they must be in a block of flats. Polished steel threw her image back at her: a woman in evening dress, her arm bent up behind her back by a middle-aged man with a spreading belly and dyed hair. She met his eyes in the reflection. They were utterly cold.

As the lift doors opened, he gave her a shove. She tottered forward out of the lift, colliding with the far wall. She was conscious of a door opening, of Nico's three men in suits disposing themselves about the corridor, and then Nico himself reached out and yanked her forward into the room.

Everything was dark to her dazzled eyes. Then she made out that she faced a wall on which the paper was peeling, illuminated dimly from outside by a street lamp.

A switch clicked.

Light flooded the room. A bare 100-watt bulb hung from the centre of the ceiling. She glanced around, seeing the peeling wallpaper clearly; the sagging single bed with a worn blanket tossed across it, and the sort of dresser and wardrobe that landlords buy at house-clearance sales to furnish their downmarket properties.

A fly-specked mirror hung skewed on the wall over the rusty sink.

'I keep this place on,' his cool voice breathed in her ear, 'just to remind me. This was mine, when I was first here. I bought the building. Soon, I will make it over and sell it. But for now – this is where a poor boy slept, dreaming of the smart English women who would not even look at him in the street. Until he began to dream what he would do to them, should he ever have one of them at his mercy.'

The shabby window curtains were not drawn. If anyone was awake in any one of the surrounding tower-block flats, they could see her as clearly as if she stood on a stage. Alix, her wrist still caught in his powerful grip and her senses overwhelmed by the smell of him, whispered, 'What did you dream you would do? What's your fantasy?'

There was a pause. When he spoke again, standing behind her, she couldn't see him, but she heard the hitch in his breathing. His grip on her wrist tightened to just short of painful.

'I think perhaps that she would look at me scornfully . . .'

Breathing hard, Alix pulled her hand out of his grip. She turned, placing her right foot in front of her left, posing catwalk-perfect for a moment in the shabby, harshly lit bedsit. With no trace of a smile, she looked him up and down.

'. . . And I would tell her to strip.'

'And if she says no?'

'Then I will tear the dress off her back.'

The real world threatened to intervene. *Not after what this dress cost me!* trembled on her lips. She stepped back, involuntarily, and saw the black pupils of his eyes dilate. Slowly, slowly, she backed away; until she felt the damp wall pressing against her shoulder-blades.

'If she was – if she was very afraid of being here – and of you – she might do what you say—'

Slowly, without taking her eyes off him, she reached up behind her back for the zip of her dress. Her fumbling fingers found it. She tugged, and it slid down. The loosening of the fabric around her made her face flame and her ears burn. The zip reached the bottom, and the dress peeled apart like a flower opening, sliding down over her hips to puddle at her feet.

She stepped forward out of it. Now she wore only stiletto heels, stockings, panties and an ivory lace suspender belt. Her small, rounded breasts did not need a bra.

The chill air of the room prickled on her skin.

'And if she were afraid—' Nico's voice broke again. She saw patches of sweat spreading on to the breast of his shirt, and a bulge in the front of his trousers. 'I would take her – like this.'

He moved forward, surprisingly lithely for a middle-aged man. Alix shivered, and stood perfectly still. Her nipples rose up with the touch of the cold air and hardened at the exposure to his gaze.

His hand reached down and grabbed the front of her panties, yanking them. The material cut into her crotch, hard and painful. She gasped. He yanked again – the panties wouldn't tear. With a hurried, 'Wait!', she dipped her hip and pulled them down herself, tangling them momentarily in her high heels.

'*Puta!*' He snatched them out of her hand and wadded them up into a ball. One of his hands cupped the back of her head where her neat hair began to fall down on her shoulders. His other hand stuffed the panties hard against her lips until she opened her mouth and his fingers forced the cloth inside.

She felt herself swung around. A moment of sheer unerotic panic overtook her – *I can't breathe!*

This might do it for some people, but not me.

She reached up and pulled the panties out of her mouth, keeping her back to him. Her ribs creaked as she breathed in. She kept her hands cupped over her face, pressing the soiled silk to her lips, inhaling the warm smell.

There was a moment of hesitation. As if Nico couldn't see what he wanted to see. There was no table in the bedsit, she realised, nothing she could be bent forward over.

Instead, with a muttered curse, he pushed her down on her face on the bed. The wool of the blanket was rough under her naked skin. She tried to roll over, and caught a glimpse of him looming above her, tearing off his jacket. A hard-on poked out the front of his trousers. Cursing and swearing, he threw the jacket down and rolled her firmly back on to her face.

The suspender belt stretched as she felt herself forced over. His weight came down hard on her back, and one hand pushed in between her and the bed and grabbed her breast. She gasped, face forced down into the blanket, crumpled knickers lost. Tears came to her eyes.

Not the pain, but the fact that he wasn't listening to her, taking notice of her – that made her cream. She felt her hot juices running over her cunt and down her thighs, slicking the smooth skin. She humped her bare arse up into his body, pressing her buttocks against his crotch. His cock thrust against her. She felt him fumble with his zip: then the naked warmth of it pressed into her skin, feeling huge, the head prodding at her labia, at her buttocks, at her arsehole.

'Take it up you, English bitch!'

Both his hands came down tight on her shoulders now. She twisted desperately, managing to turn her head on one side and breathe.

He didn't notice. Now his full flabby weight was on her and his knees were between hers, pushing her thighs apart. She felt his cock brush tantalisingly over her swollen flesh. Her hips jerked, attempting to force herself up on to him.

'No!'

She felt him free a hand, reach back to grab the shaft of his cock and steer the head. Again, it brushed her swelling, hot, juicy labia. Helpless, she writhed against him. She felt the swollen head of his cock hesitate, then push between her buttocks. It pressed at her arsehole, and she gasped aloud.

His hand swept across her cunt, spreading the lubrication of her own juices. She felt him slather his cock in her, wetting it. Then he lifted his hips, and drove down – plunging the head of his cock into her back passage. She shrieked out loud, feeling him force through the ring of muscle. A searing pain: then a giving, as she forced herself to relax her sphincter muscles. He slid an inch or two in.

Nico froze. Alix lay on her stomach, legs spread wide, impaled on the head of his cock. Her arse felt full to bursting. Tears ran out of her eyes: she didn't know whether of pleasure or pain. *If he pushes further up me—! Oh God. Good thing he's thin!* She almost burst out into wild laughter.

The flesh that impaled her twitched. She felt him shift his grip back to her hips, and lift his body as if to thrust hard up her—

A spurt of red-hot liquid filled her arse. Nico sank down over her with a groan. Full weight, now; none of it taken by his arms, and she grunted, wriggling, to no avail. She felt his cock begin to shrink and slide out of her.

But here I am.

At that realisation, and utterly to her surprise, her own flesh convulsed. The cheap room, the middle-aged man, the sleaziness: all of it somehow combined in her head and shot through her cunt, a spike of pleasure that throbbed to be released again and again. She shifted her body, pressing herself down into the rough blanket. The harsh wool ground against her sensitive swollen clit. Pleasure spiked again through her vaginal walls, a searing orgasm that was nothing to do with the man on top of her; that was not a mind-obliterating ecstasy, but a sharp, triumphant jolt.

At last she lay still.

The air began to chill her sweaty flesh. Above her, Nico shifted and slid down, laying half on top of her and half beside her. She was about to speak when she heard a small snore coming from him.

And I never did find out where the bathroom is in this place . . .

Towards dawn, she slid out from under him, and off the bed; washing amateurishly in the sink, and dressing herself as well as she could. With her arms up as she did her hair, she met her own gaze in the mirror. She grinned, half triumphant, half rueful.

The advantage of fantasy is that there's no clearing up afterwards. No awkward hellos and goodbyes. It's all just . . . gone.

Chapter Seven

THE PUB HALF A mile down the road from the college had become a student hang-out by default. Alix hesitated as she came up to it, and then signalled and swung the big car into the car park outside. A slow heat hung over the morning, and her thoughts were still lazy from the night before.

She winced as she moved on the leather upholstery, shifting her foot from the accelerator to the brake. A very unromantic soreness made her arse flinch. But a secretive smile came to her face.

I actually did it. Not a fantasy: I *did* it . . .

He doesn't know who I am or where I live. He didn't even ask for my false name. He didn't take me anywhere I'll recognise. I'm safe, I think. Unless I go down the Marquis, I won't see him again.

I could do that, she mused. I could see him again. There's the attraction of power and danger, of course. But – does that work, now I know he's actually a rather nice man?

The thought of calling Nico 'nice' to his face made her grin and shake her head.

And he may be vulnerable in bed, but he's dodgy and dangerous outside it. And . . . last night was one mood. Suppose the next time he decides to beat me up? Or not let me leave?

She got out of the car, the heat hitting her like a blow after the cool of the air-conditioning. Air shimmered and danced over the hot metal of the car roof, and heat burned her fingertips as she closed the door behind her.

'Time for coffee, anyhow,' she murmured to herself, glancing at her watch. And possibly some of the Yannis Road crowd would be inside, before lectures. *I want to ask Fern how she's getting on with her . . . experiences.*

The change from sunlight to the interior of the bar confused her. Disorientated, she paused for a moment, with the harsh light behind her. In front of her, a figure came clear in the gloom – her own image in the mirror behind the bar. A young woman with silver-fair hair caught up in a ponytail, dressed in a pearl-coloured singlet top and a long silky grey skirt. Haloed by the light . . . Newly confident.

There is no substitute for real *risk*.

Stepping down into the room, she walked carefully ahead to the bar, still a little dazzled.

'Orange and lemonade, please.' She leaned back on the polished wood, the sunlight from outside the pub windows now illuminating the interior. There were none of the students she recognised in the desultory groups seated on the black-painted benches. A tall fair-haired man was leaning on the bar beside her. He lifted his head and her heart lurched, recognising Sandro Elliot.

The arrival of her drink, and paying for it, gave her a second to collect her mind. Her fingers fumbled the change. She sipped the top of the fizzy liquid quickly, in case her shaking hand should spill it. *Dear God, I want him so much I can't breathe!*

Even if, right now, I don't *like* him very much.

'Go on,' she said suddenly, exasperated, 'walk out, why don't you? You make it plain enough you don't want to be in the same building as me, never mind the same room!'

He turned towards her, looking down at her from his greater height. His jaw showed clean-shaven, and the sun picked out the heaviness of his fair brows and the deepness of the blue of his eyes. There was no expression on his face that she could make out – almost, she would have thought he didn't see her.

'Alix. Hi. How are you managing with your – with Professor Mayhew's project?' He smiled, and she saw his strong white teeth for a second. 'It's going well in the control group. Women getting in touch with their deepest, most desirable fantasies; becoming *real* women . . .'

His voice was smooth, urbane; as if she hadn't just told him, in so many words, to get lost. Alix shook her head.

'I'm not one of your students,' she said. 'I'm a businesswoman; I've been out in the world. So don't try to con me, *Mister* Elliot. You don't like me, do you?'

'Not like you?' His deep voice rose a little, as if startled.

'What do you usually call it when you don't want to sleep with a woman?' Alix asked sarcastically. 'Professor Vivienne says you're not gay. You're not married. That doesn't leave much!'

He made to move away. Alix shifted forward off the bar, catching at his arm. He was wearing a short-sleeved shirt, and her hand closed around his bare lower arm, below his elbow. Soft blond hair brushed her palm, and she felt the movement of rock-hard muscles under his tanned skin. The scent of him came to her: masculine sweat and air-dried cotton. She felt her inner walls loosen with desire.

'And what's all this crap about "real women"?' she demanded, exasperated. 'What do you think *I* am?'

The American looked down at her hand on his arm. She almost expected him to pick it off like a troublesome insect; shoo her away like an importunate cat. Sandro Elliot did neither. She could feel his tension through his muscles.

This is freaking him out as much as it is me! Why?

The warmth of his skin felt beautiful under her hand. While he didn't move, she breathed in, drawing in his scent. No aftershave, no cologne; nothing but the particular scent of his own, extremely masculine, body. Slowly, lightly, she slid her palm up his forearm a little, then down towards his broad wrist and the leather strap of his watch; then up again . . .

She felt small, standing beside the tall man. And, athletic as she was, she felt frail. *I work out in the gym, but with him it's natural, isn't it?* An impulse to put her arms around his neck came to her, and she barely managed to suppress it. Now she traced with her fingertips the contours of his arm, muscles and tendons; and the warm flesh prickled under her hand, all the blond hairs standing up.

'I'm a student here, but I'm not one of your students . . . it isn't that simple, is it? That I'm a student?'

'You're just a *girl*. I—' His voice cracked.

Alix glanced down. The fly of his worn pale jeans was bulging. For a second she stared in sheer disbelief. Slowly, she lowered her hand from his arm and closed it over his crotch. The warm denim moved under her palm as his cock leaped.

'I thought you didn't like me,' she murmured, amazed. 'Sandro, what is it? Why don't we—'

'Excuse me. Excuse me!' In one second he turned

away from her, leaving her hand cold and empty; swept the briefcase off the bar and held it in front of him, and all but staggered towards the door, hunched over. The door banged behind him as he lurched out into sunlight.

I don't get it!

She became aware that a smile was curving her mouth; that a delicious joy flushed through her, heating her, making her want to dance with delight.

He *does* want me! He does, he does, he does!

His body can't lie. He wants me, all right. But . . .

Alix slowly stopped smiling.

. . . But he doesn't *want* to want me.

Why? Am I not good enough for him? What is it that I don't do?

Or is it what I don't do *yet*? Is he waiting for me to learn something – get in touch with these 'deepest desires' he's always on about? Because if he is . . . I don't know what they are.

The altercation at the bar had gone unnoticed, she saw. Students caught up in their own lives and dramas. She drained the rest of her drink. A dull headache started behind her eyes.

Maybe . . . Maybe I'll just skip the lecture today. I wish I could talk to somebody. Not Professor Vivienne: she has to work with him, it's too embarrassing. Maybe . . . I'll go and see if Fern is at the house.

If anyone will have an idea, she will!

By the time Alix got to Yannis Road, the headache was bad enough that she could barely drive. Fern Barrie came out and led her into the house, into the welcome cool, and got her water from the fridge.

'Lie down for an hour,' Fern recommended. 'On the sofa. Or you can use my room if you like. Nobody's home until the afternoon today, so it'll be quiet.'

'Thanks.' Alix pressed the back of her hand against her forehead. The flesh felt stretched, strained, hot. 'It's mostly dehydration, I think. Could I have some more water? And if you don't mind, I will try and sleep for an hour.'

The Yannis Road house had obviously been rented from an upmarket agency – one or other of the students must have parents with money. Fern Barrie's bedroom was painted in cream, with a big picture window overlooking the garden. The wall at the foot of the bed was one long line of fitted wardrobes, all with mirror-doors.

Alix pushed aside a pair of engineer boots and some crumpled jeans, and sat down on top of the duvet. Her head throbbed. Light reflecting in off the mirrors didn't help. She pushed the duvet back, slipped off her sandals, and lay down into the welcome firmness of the mattress, closing her eyes against brightness and pain. Eyes still shut, she clumsily stripped off her remaining clothes.

She did not expect to sleep, but she did.

Waking some indeterminate time later, she lay in a pleasurable stupor for a while, enjoying the lack of pain. The headache was gone. Noon sunlight bounced back from the wardrobe mirrors, but now she just appreciated how bright it made the room.

She found the bathroom, and then came back. The window opened easily, letting in a scent of fresh-cut grass. Knowing she should go on to college, she nonetheless felt a desire to sleep again. *Why am I so tired?*

She smiled, then. *Last night couldn't have anything to do with it, could it?*

The breeze from outside stirred the curtains. Alix lay back down on the bed. Just a few minutes, she promised herself. A delicious drowsiness spread through her body.

Nico: now, that was something . . .

Her hand strayed to her pussy. With one foot, she pushed the duvet all the way off the bed. The mirrors now reflected her body unobstructed. She drew up one knee, watching the woman in the mirror. She fingered her cunt, seeing pink flesh between straw-coloured pussy hair, darker than the hair on her head. Tremors of pleasure shuddered through her flesh.

I wonder if. . . ?

Alix rolled over on her stomach to reach the bedside table. A lamp, a clock-radio and a paperback with a broken spine took up all the available room. She hung half over the edge of the bed to open the cupboard underneath, and the drawer.

Right!

Her rummaging fingers touched hard plastic. And then a soft-textured plastic and more different shapes . . . Alix hauled them out, rolling back into the middle of the bed. She examined what she'd found.

I thought Fern might have something like this . . . And she keeps her toys clean, too . . .

Alix picked up a short, ivory-coloured dildo. Only about six inches long, the shaft was ribbed. She pressed the stud and it whirred into life – quietly: you would not hear it if you were outside the room. Ideal.

Leaning back against the headboard, she replayed Nico in her mind. The way his hand closed across her mouth in the car, pushing her back against the headrest—

She caressed the insides of her thighs with the vibrator. A loosening feeling spread through them, muscles weakening. She teased herself, running the blunt point of the dildo up her groin, over the top of her mound of Venus and back down between her legs, not touching her lips. The warmth of her groin grew hotter. A spark of fierce wanting grew in her cunt. Switching the vibrator to a higher speed, she trailed it lightly up her labia. She felt her clit swell in its hood and moved the dildo there, playing first with the tip, then with the shaft, rolling it against the hood of her clit, moving it up and down, picturing Nico's hard-on as he pushed her down on the bed—

Fire seared through her: pleasure throbbing through her clit, pulsing through her groin, her thighs, her belly. She lifted the vibrator off her flesh.

We're not done yet . . .

The next one of Fern's toys made her smile: a thick, bright pink plastic dildo, with a transparent section full of rolling balls and a vibrating clit-tickler in the shape of a rabbit with extended ears. She found herself smiling and shaking her head. She put it down and picked up the next one: a thick, black, lifelike plastic cock.

It vibrated harder, with a deeper note. She gripped it around the shaft with her hand. It had realistic veins moulded into the surface. The texture was soft, smooth, but not in any way like hot, real flesh.

She turned it up a notch and put it between her thighs, closing her legs together. She felt the vibrations through her thighs, her pelvis, her belly . . . her cunt throbbed, the walls widening. She moved her legs apart and played the tip of the plastic cock's head over her lips, feeling the shivers of her inner flesh gather in intensity. She sat further forward and looked in the mirror to guide her hand as she moved the dildo upright, poising it over her labia.

And Nico, not fucking me, making me take it up the arse—

With a sudden, deliberately brutal push, she shoved

the black cock dildo up her fanny. As her flesh engulfed the thick bulk, she came, instantly; scalding pleasure flooding her. Hot wet juices flowed around the head of the vibrating cock, lubricating her, making her wet enough to slide it inside her, leaning forward over her belly and sliding it up and down, up and down, taking more and more of it inside her, until she came again explosively, letting go and falling back against the headboard, her convulsing flesh pushing the dildo right back out.

'Ah, wow . . .' she breathed.

A layer of sweat covered her skin. Her fine hair stuck to her cheeks, her neck; her warm, wet shoulders. She wiped it back with her hands, seeing how the woman in the mirror was flushed pink from breasts to face.

The door glided open. A voice said quietly, 'Hey, you awake? – oh.'

'I – er—' Alix sat up fast, sweeping a pillow into her lap and hugging it to herself, her face fiery red. 'Fern. Hi. I didn't know you were upstairs.'

A slow cheeky smile spread over the girl's face. She came fully into the room. She was wearing her leather jacket and leather trousers, and the flush on her cheeks might have been from riding the bike, or it might not.

'I went out to get some milk,' Fern said. 'I thought you'd be all right. I guess you are!'

'Er, well, yeah. I guess.' Alix found herself blushing again.

'Hey, don't worry about it. You coulda asked me, but hey, share and share alike, yeah?' Fern plumped herself down on the mattress, still looking at Alix. Her little pink lips curved into a wicked grin, showing her even white teeth. Her eyes gleamed.

'What were you getting off on?' she asked.

Alix cuddled the pillow closer to her naked breasts.

The presence of an uninvited person should have shocked her out of her erotic daze, if only through embarrassment, but instead she felt herself getting hotter.

'I was thinking of this guy who fucked me last night,' she confessed. 'Fern, do you ... get off, afterwards, with the fantasies you're doing for real?'

The girl nodded, soberly. Her eyes still gleamed. She had a little purple eyeshadow on, making her sharp little face seem biker-slutty. She reached up and pulled her zip down, letting her leather jacket slide back down off her shoulders.

'Oh yeah,' Fern said, 'I do. It's not like anything else, this, is it? Sometimes I think it's doing my head in.'

'You too?' Alix felt a flood of relief. 'I'm glad it's not just me! It's not that I'm not enjoying it. It just ... all seems to be happening so quickly. And I was celibate for a long time before this. I think I'd got out of the habit.'

The girl grinned roguishly. 'I dunno, you looked in practice to me!'

Alix brought her hands up to cover and cool her cheeks. 'Look, I *am* sorry ...' She blew out a long breath. 'I just can't seem to think about anything else. God knows how I'm going to pass my course!'

The abandoned leather jacket smelled like satchels to Alix, and the first day of school, as well as bike rides with boyfriends. As she watched, Fern stood up and turned away toward the wardrobes. She opened one, taking out a dress on a hanger, and hooked it over the top of the door.

'I'm going out with Joley,' Fern said, glancing back over her shoulder. Her hands moved in front of her: Alix could hear her unzip her leather trousers. Fern's hands slid under her trousers, easing them down over her hips, and she took them off, standing up in only her white panties and T-shirt. As Alix carried on staring, Fern stripped off the shirt, unsnapped her tiny white bra and turned around. Naked except for her panties.

'I'm not going out for a while, though,' she said.

The sun through the window shone on her untidy soft spikes of hair, lighting up a mole high on her cheekbone. She wasn't wearing her lip-piercing, Alix saw. Its absence left the emphasis on her mouth: wide, soft, with smile-curves at each corner.

'Are you going to go on hiding behind that pillow?' she added.

Alix laughed, spreading her hands and letting the pillow fall away. She shook her head ruefully. 'You see what I mean about things going too fast for me? My body's way ahead of me here. I don't know if I can take this.'

The girl's face fell. For a moment she looked solemn, hurt. 'But . . . we're friends, aren't we? And besides, I propositioned you before we ever got involved with the Professor!'

'Yes. Yes, you did.' Alix pushed the pillow away, enjoying the breeze from the open window on her naked skin. 'I didn't know you were serious.'

'Yes, you did,' Fern contradicted. She sat down on the end of the bed. 'I've always had a thing for older women. It's not like I want us to be girlfriends or anything, but *friends* – why are you laughing at me?'

' "Older women"!' Alix spluttered. She fell over sideways on the bed, making little squeaking noises. 'Older – oh! That hurts my ribs. Oh . . . Thanks for the compliment!'

She was aware of the girl rolling over, until they were lying facing each other on the bed. Fern's trim body was the palest golden colour, her tiny round breasts crowned with strawberry-pink nipples. Her flat belly had a silver ring piercing her navel. Her smooth hips flared narrowly, and flowed into long, lithe legs. She was not skinny or frail, Alix saw with pleasure; a junior athlete's body, maybe. Healthy and firm. And lively . . .

'Do you want me to?' Alix asked.

'Yes. Only if *you* want to, though.'

A feeling of relaxation went through Alix. *At least I won't have to write this one up afterwards!* She reached out and ruffled the younger woman's hair, then trailed her fingers down over the sharp little chin, and stroked the firm curve of Fern's breast. *Which I've been wanting to do since I saw her in the café,* she admitted to herself.

'You've got some collection here,' Alix added.

'Oh, well, you know what it's like. You keep seeing a different version in the shops . . .' Fern looked down at Alix's hand on her breast, smiling. She picked up another one of the vibrators, another plastic cylinder, about as thick as a medium-sized cock. Alix saw the shape was a stylised cock, with a v-shaped bulge for a head, wide enough to fill the entrance of a vagina.

A low humming filled the air. Fern switched the vibrator to a medium setting, stroking it down her own belly. The silver ring in her navel blurred, shaking with the vibrations. She giggled, and slid the tip of the dildo further down, lifting one knee.

'You going to help me with this?' Fern said. 'You want to fuck my arse with this dildo?'

'It's not your arse I want this time.' Alix became aware her voice was coming out thick. Heat flared through her flesh, warming her out to her fingertips. 'I want your pussy.'

A brilliant, teasing smile. 'Hey, whatever!'

Alix reached out, enclosing Fern's hand in her own.

The vibrations slid through their flesh together. She took the pink plastic dildo, kneeling up on the bed, seeing both of them in the wardrobe mirrors – a short-haired, tiny girl with her legs sprawled apart, naked except for white panties. Alix herself with her hair tumbling down and hiding her firm breasts.

'I'm going to shove this right up you!' Alix said.

'Do it! I'm wet just hearing you!' The girl reached down and hitched the gusset of her panties aside. Alix stared at her evenly tanned flesh. Fern put her first two fingers between her labia and spread them. Alix feasted her eyes on the pink flesh, the nub of the clitoris sliding under its hood. Glistening liquid ran down and soaked the white cotton.

'You don't need these.' Alix reached forward and slid her free hand under the girl's buttocks. They were warm and firm. She grabbed the thin cotton in her fist and pulled, dragging the knickers down Fern's legs until they stretched and stopped, caught by her spread thighs.

The girl let her head fall back, gazing up at Alix. She reached up and closed her hands over Alix's breasts, digging her fingers into each tit. The pain of it brought her nipples up hard, and she gasped. Immediately the hands shifted to kneading, rubbing, smoothing her flesh.

'You want this up you?' Alix trailed the dildo down Fern's belly, brought it up to circle the pink nipples and bring them to instant peaks; slowly brought it down between her breasts, over her flat tummy, and down between her legs. The girl's pubic hair was shaved in a little dark vertical stripe. Moisture glistened in the springy curls.

'Yes!' Fern gasped. 'Yes, yes, *yes*!'

Alix grunted. Fire burned: she was a furnace

between her legs. She thrust herself down, writhing against the girl's hands where they gripped her tits. She knelt up, looking down at the spread thighs beneath her. The thickness of the vibrator filled her hand.

Tantalisingly, she touched the very tip to the girl's lips. Fern's hips bucked off the bed. Alix gasped as the grip on her breasts tightened. She stroked the vibrator up between Fern's thighs; up and down; teasing until the hot liquid running down the shaft lubricated the buzzing dildo thoroughly. She felt her own cunt dripping, juices running down her thighs. Briefly she left Fern's pussy to stroke the vibrator between her own legs. The girl arched up under her, body craving the sensation.

Alix shifted her grip, taking a fistful of the dildo far down the shaft. She poised her hand for a minute, meeting Fern's heavy-lidded gaze. The younger woman gasped, breathing heavily, almost panting. Alix took a firm grip, stroked the tip of the dildo between the woman's inner lips, and pushed. There was a momentary resistance; then the flesh parted, and she thrust into sticky hot darkness.

Fern's hands left her breasts. Alix, panting, worked the shaft of the vibrator round, making sure that all the surfaces of the inner walls were drenched in the sensation. Fern began to thrust against her hand. She matched the rhythm, pressing her thighs together in the same way; speeded up a little, speeded up some more; her hand pumping the thick plastic cock deep into the girl's body, pumping, thrusting, and then pushing it forward so that the shaft vibrated full against the hood of her clitoris.

With a scream, the short-haired girl came, her body rearing up off the bed. Alix dropped the dildo. She threw her arms around the plump golden hips in front of her, dropped her face into Fern's crotch and licked and sucked at the salty deliciousness of her searing-hot flesh. Fern went limp for a moment, then tensed and came again with a breathless yell.

They sank down on the bed beside each other.

'Oh, wow, you're *good*.' Fern evidently couldn't get her breath. 'You know what I like!'

Alix, her hands shaking, couldn't say a word. She ached in her fanny, ached with wanting to come.

'I tell you what!' The younger woman bounced up on the bed. 'Why don't I show you what I'm going to be wearing when I go out?'

'This is no time to appeal to my dress-sense!' Alix swore under her breath. A haze of desire possessed her. She put her hand down between her legs, pressing solidly against her clit. Her pussy hair was soaked with hot liquid; she felt it trickling out of her. *Oh God, I want to come—*

Inside seconds, Fern had discarded her panties, shown Alix a pert rounded bottom as she rummaged in the wardrobe, and emerged with a dress that she threw on over her head and wriggled into.

It was velvet, Alix saw. A rich, lilac velvet; made into a close-fitting dress that slid wonderfully down the younger woman's slender-waisted body. It hung all the better for Alix knowing that Fern wasn't wearing any knickers. It was a simple style, with full-length close-fitting sleeves, and cut in a low, wide square neck.

'How about this?' Fern's eyes danced. She sat herself on the bed beside Alix, clasping her hands over her velvet-covered bodice and pushing her breasts up into a magnificent cleavage, arching her neck back, and looking under her lashes in best sultry-movie-star fashion. 'Like what you see?'

Rich shadows collected in the folds of material

around her neat hips. Her fingers peeped out from under the ends of her long sleeves. And the packed bodice, Alix thought . . .

'Yeah, I like it,' she growled. 'Now fuck me, damn it!'

The girl met her eye. Keeping eye contact, and with a blazing mischievous grin, Fern slid down on to her knees beside the bed, tugging at Alix to stand up.

Alix's knees were rubbery; she found herself barely able to stand. Looking down, she could see straight down Fern's bodice to her erect nipples under the velvet. Looking in the mirror, she could see herself stark-bollock-naked, with a woman kneeling at her feet.

As she watched the reflection, she saw Fern pick up the thick black plastic cock. The girl's hand shoved her thighs further apart, and Alix had to drop her hands to Fern's shoulders to steady herself. She watched the girl sliding the vibrator up her inner thigh, at the same time that she felt it; both sensations together made her insides melt and flood.

With an endearing clumsiness, the younger woman pushed the head of the dildo firmly up Alix's cunt. Alix breathed in, tightening her grip on Fern's sweating shoulders. She felt herself opened, parted; the gradual friction speeding up, speeding up—

With a gush of juice, she came; scalding pleasure darting through her cunt and belly, shaking her body thunderously. Her knees gave and she slid down beside Fern, conscious of the vibrator being removed and Fern's small hand sliding over her mound to take its place. The light pressure of those fingers made her orgasm again. Speechless, she shut her eyes, and tried to stop her heaving breaths.

'Oh *Jesus*!' she yelped. 'You're not so bad yourself . . .'

She felt Fern's lips press her own, lightly. When she opened her eyes, it was to see the girl smiling at her.

'Think of it as a rest,' Fern advised. 'We can do this when we're tired of doing Professor Mayhew's stuff.'

'A rest!'

'Well, you know what I mean . . .' Fern Barrie pushed herself upright, and sprawled over on to the bed. She patted the mattress. Alix, groaning under her breath, pushed her body up and flopped down beside the girl. Fern hooked one leg companionably over Alix's knee.

'I know what you mean,' Alix said. 'Yes. It sort of . . . grounds me.'

'Me too.'

The heat of the sun outside kept her from being chilly as the sweat dried on her body. Alix rolled over and propped herself up on one elbow.

'I think I've got a better handle on this now,' she said. 'As for the Professor . . . this probably means I can carry on. I want to. But then, there's Sandro Elliot.'

'Elliot's a problem?' Fern's bright eyes widened.

'Oh yes. Yes, he is . . .'

Chapter Eight

'... *BUT I STILL DON'T* know what he's waiting for me to find out! What is a "real woman" anyway, if I'm not it? And what is it with *him* – I know he wants me!' Alix finished, halfway between a whine and exasperation. 'Oh, listen to me. I should just shut up about him, right?'

Fern sprawled across the counterpane, naked again, utterly unselfconscious. The sunlight dappled the smooth skin of her legs and buttocks, and the pink folds of her sex. She let her head roll back, leaning over the edge of the bed and staring upside down out of the window.

'Hey, things look really weird this way ... Yes, you should shut up about him. But you won't! Hey, did he really get a stiffie?'

Alix sat up slowly, pulling her dress on over her head. She emerged flushed, hair tumbled in a sweat-sticky mass. 'Oh, he did. He *definitely* did.'

'Maybe he *does* think you're going to find out you like – I dunno, sex with sheep! – and turn into a super-lay.' Fern giggled, stretching out her skinny arms. She rolled over on to her stomach, grinning up at Alix from under her gamin-cut brown hair. 'Who knows what men think? Most of the time, they think with the little head, not the big one.'

It was too hot to dress, Alix decided. She stripped the cotton frock off again. *And I could do with a shower*.

'Fern, how *are* you getting on?' she asked.

' "Getting on"?'

'You know, with the project. The fantasies. When you do them for real...' Alix waited. After a few seconds Fern sat up on the bed, wrapping her arms around her elbows, still grinning. A faint sheen of sweat still covered her breasts. Her little pink labia were still flushed.

'You want to hear all about it ... Just like Joley and Robbie and Adam!'

Alix shook her head. 'No ... Well, I do, but it's ... I want to know if there's something I'm missing. Maybe there *is* a fantasy in the back of my mind that would just, I don't know, change everything, make me superorgasmic ... So I want to know just, how are you "getting on" ...'

'You mean, is it different?' Fern's expression became more serious – wired, even. 'Oh, yes. But it's like difficult to say how, you know? Oh, look, I'll just tell you, shall I? I did my first one this weekend, 'cos it's the first time I've really been away from college this term ...'

The ticking of the bike engine died down to silence. Fern Barrie slid the bike on to its stand. She dismounted and took off her lid, letting the summer air blow through her short, sweaty hair, cooling her down.

Where am I? Haven't seen a signpost for miles...

Getting lost had not been entirely easy, but she'd come a hundred miles or more away from the capital, and could say only that this must be the southern coast *some*where. There would be towns over the horizons, and holiday traffic; but none of that here . . .

Behind her, low trees and scrub covered a rise. In front, the waters of the English Channel sparkled and danced. Dazzling light glittered. She wiped her hand across her forehead, feeling hot in her leathers now the chill of riding the bike had gone.

A pebbled beach curved away on either side. Fern grinned to herself. *If this was my real fantasy, it would either be totally deserted, or covered completely in nude men! There certainly wouldn't be some old guys walking their dogs . . .*

Her body sweated inside the heavy jacket and leather trousers. She narrowed her eyes against the glare. The figures walking their dogs further down the beach seemed distant and tiny – but that might be deceptive and they might be here quicker than she thought. She eyed the water again, where the low waves spluttered white on to grey pebbles, and the smell of salt stuck in her nostrils.

It doesn't matter where you are, you can't reach fantasyland . . .

Jesus God, I need a piss!

Fern put the bike helmet in the pannier and straightened up, looking for concealing bushes. There were none. She looked at the bike, and then back at the slope behind, and then decisively began to lope up the low hill, her boots sliding deep into the scree.

What was underfoot changed in a few yards to scrub, and then to low violet-coloured heather. She took in deep breaths as she staggered towards the top of the rise. It was hard going. The sweet scent of the heather made her almost dizzy.

Topping the rise, she found herself overlooking a swathe of countryside, mauve with heather, and dotted with the occasional yellow-flowering gorse bush. The ground gave way squelchily under her feet.

Fern stood, turning on the spot, squinting against the sun . . . nobody here, but there wouldn't be: heathland is hard unless you're a dedicated backpacker, and even then you'd stick to the paths.

So I may have found my deserted country. But what's the point? I can lie down and finger-fuck, but it's hardly megafantasy, is it?

As she completed her turn, she saw with relief that towards the east there were trees and green grass where the ground went down to a cleft. A few minutes of scrambling brought her there, under the pale green leaves of beeches. She heard a stream running over rocks at the base of the cleft. The sunlight fell in shafts through the low trees. The grass was cropped short – not by people: there were spatters of dried rabbit-droppings here and there.

Fern reached up and unzipped her leather jacket. She laid it across the outflung branch of one of the trees. Cool air touched her arms, her shoulders and her sweat-soaked black T-shirt. She felt all the fine hairs on her skin standing up. A few distant insects buzzed.

Physically uncomfortable – and made more so by the sound of the running water – Fern reached down, unzipped the heavy lined leather trousers, and slipped them down her legs. She tugged her boots off, one at a time, staggering on one leg; then pulled off the trousers completely and jumped down on to the flat stones in the stream bed, yelping quietly under her breath.

The stones were sun-warmed. She stood with her left foot on one and her right on another, and reached down with her fingers to pull the gusset of her panties aside. Sighing with relief she let a golden stream go, and watched it fall into the river, steaming a little in the cool air under the trees.

A male voice close at hand said *'Wow!'* and whistled loudly.

'Son of a *bitch*!' Startled, Fern let go of her knickers, spraying her hands and the cloth with piss; staggered two steps sideways on the flat stones, and felt her foot skid on the wet surface. She threw her arms wide, grabbed a tree branch, and sat down heavily in the river shallows.

'*Fuck!*' she added, shaking her head, half-blinded by the spray.

The stream was surprisingly cold. She stood up, water cascading down her legs. Droplets flew as she looked rapidly around, trying to see who had spoken and where they were. The bushes between the trees rustled.

'And you can fucking come out of *there*!' Fern bellowed. She climbed back up on to the bank of the stream, her knickers and T-shirt clinging clammily to her skin. Swearing under her breath, she reached down, peeled her wet panties off, and slung them from one of the branches. Then she pulled off her T-shirt, trying to use the dry part to wipe down her slender, pale body.

Either the cold water or knowing that she must be being watched made her pink nipples stand out stark and rock-hard.

'I know you're there . . .' A slight shiver made her teeth chatter. She looked at her dry leathers, hanging invitingly on the tree branch. The jacket felt heavy when she picked it up and slung it around her shoulders.

Maybe they left, she thought, disconsolate.

Well, of course they did – this is real life. They realised they'd surprised somebody, saw a half-naked woman and ran like hell! Afraid of getting into trouble. Ah, shit . . .

A dry branch cracked.

Fern found that her mouth was dry. She held the jacket together over her breasts. It hung down low enough to just cover the shaved strip of her pussy hair, but if she moved . . .

Just my luck. Looking for a porno-movie scene, and I've probably found the local axe-murderer.

'I've got a cellphone,' she said loudly and coolly. 'You can bugger off if you don't want to be here when the cops arrive.'

'You 'ave to tell them where you are first,' a voice remarked – and not the same voice, she realised, her hands shaking. This one had a slight Welsh accent – and it was also male. 'We've been lost most of the day . . .'

'You leave her alone, or I'll have you!' a third voice interjected. And this one, Fern realised, was female.

'Will you fucking come out where I can see you!' Fern snapped, temper carrying her away. There was movement in the bushes.

She hadn't seen them, she realised, because she'd been looking at eye level. The bodies that rolled over and appeared out of nowhere were wearing camouflage clothing, and had been under the edges of the bushes. A dark-skinned man stood up, then two more, both with shaved heads; a thick-set man; two indeterminate blonds – and the second of those had hair up in a neat bun and so must be the female voice, Fern realised.

'Out on exercise,' she murmured, not making it a question. They looked much her age; the woman maybe a year or two older, and the more muscled of the shaven-headed men had a touch of puppy fat to him still.

The blonde woman in the green combats said, 'Sorry

about this, miss. You stumbled in on us. We're doing escape and evasion.'

Fern slowly began to smile. She looked the woman up and down. Though the clothing did much to disguise it, the blonde was very well put together – her belt nipped in to emphasise her narrow waist, and her breasts strained against the mud-stained combat jacket. That, compared with the cool formality of her uniform . . .

The air under the trees ruffled Fern's hair, drying the water-droplets on her skin. She loosened her hold on the leather jacket. It slid a little apart. By the way each man's eyes left hers and their gazes riveted at her crotch, she guessed they could see her pussy hair. She let the jacket open even more. The dark soldier licked his lips, staring at her small, rounded breasts, and her erect nipples.

'Um, you ought to go, miss,' the woman said.

I need the right words, Fern thought, looking at the faces. *The right words so this doesn't turn nasty – and so it doesn't vanish either.*

'Hey,' she smiled slowly, 'have you guys ever pulled a train?'

The taller of the shaven-headed soldiers coughed, startled. His mate grinned. The two of them shuffled a bit, looking at each other.

'Welll . . .'

'Well, do you want to?' Fern let the jacket go and put one fist on her hip. She felt deliciously exposed, and couldn't help preening for them, turning a little to one side and letting a shaft of sunlight gleam white from her arm and breast and belly, and the long smooth expanse of her thigh. She let her other hand lie over her stomach, her middle finger pushing at the tops of her labia.

'Oh fuck!' the shaven-headed boy exclaimed – he couldn't have been more than twenty, she thought; not much older than her, and despite the uniform's attempt to make him interchangeable with everyone else, he had strong, tanned features and wonderfully blue eyes. *What's in those pants?* she wondered.

As she lowered her gaze, she saw the growing bulge in his uniform trousers.

'Miss, you didn't ought to do this.' The woman sounded uncomfortable.

Not for me, Fern thought. For her. She thinks if they fuck me, they might look at her differently.

'We could start, you and me,' Fern offered. A blush suffused the woman's cheeks. Her long lashes lowered over her eyes. She shook her head.

'But then, nobody has to do anything they don't want to. You could keep lookout,' Fern offered.

'Okay. If you're sure you . . .' The woman looked around at the other soldiers. Something in their expressions that Fern couldn't read obviously got to her. Suddenly she grinned – a strutting, piratical grin that sent a pulse of arousal through Fern's groin – and strode across the short grass.

'If you guys are going to pull a train,' she said, 'you're going to need something to get the engine running . . .'

The woman reached up and pulled at her bun. Brown-blonde hair flowed down over her shoulders, changing the shape of her face. Fern noticed her soft, full, red lips, just as the woman reached out and put her hand to the back of Fern's head, and jammed her mouth against Fern's.

A hot sensation shot from her mouth to her groin. Fern grabbed the woman's shoulders, pressing herself against the whole length of the woman's body. The webbing and belt got in the way, but she hardly noticed the straps grazing her bare skin. The jacket fell away, leaving her naked. The woman's hot tongue in her mouth leaped, intertwining with her own. Thrusting, drawing back to tease; hot lips sucking at hers . . .

With a breathless gasp, Fern broke free.

'Wow . . .' she breathed. She wasn't entirely certain, but she thought some of the men standing watching said the same. Over the woman's shoulder, her eyes met those of the Afro-Caribbean soldier. He had his hand in his fly, closed around his thick dark cock, moving his fingers gently as he kept his eyes fixed on the two women.

'You sure?' the woman said. Then she frowned. 'You going to ask my boys for money?'

'For – *no*. I'm not a whore. I'm doing this 'cos I always wanted to – and who knows when there'll be another chance like *this*?'

The woman nodded, satisfied. She ran her hand up Fern's flank. Her cool, dirt-ingrained skin felt rough. As she moved her hand up to cup Fern's breast, Fern felt her whole tit tightening and engorging. Breath caught in her throat, and she gasped.

'Nobody's going to be down this way for at least an hour,' the woman soldier said. 'If we get caught, I never heard of you, right?'

'Right.'

'But if you're sure . . .'

'You goin' to leave us to it, Corp?' the dark-haired man with the Welsh accent asked. He was almost unconsciously rubbing his hand across his fly, and the bulge of his erection was packing his pants.

'Shame!' The other one of the shaven-headed soldiers – hair cropped close enough to almost look bald, ears sticking out – grinned. 'I'd pay money to watch you 'ave her first, Corp!'

'I bet you would, Johnson.' The woman's voice was cool. She reached up, redoing her hair as she spoke. Only Fern was near enough to see the shaking of her fingers and feel the heat of desire coming off her. 'You don't know shit, do you? The army teaches discipline. The lady here wants you to oblige her. So I'm going to see that you do. Each and every one of you. Is that clear?'

It was exactly the right tone, Fern saw. Close to real life, but far enough from it to free them into the fantasy. *And now we don't give them any more time to think about it.*

'Johnson: you first!'

'Yes, ma'am!'

Fern turned away, picked up her leather jacket, and spread it on the grass. The sun glinted in through the trees. The cool air made her skin begin to goosepimple as she lowered herself down and spread her legs on the ground. The warm lining of the jacket kept her back from the chill grass.

She reached up as the shaven-headed Johnson walked over and stood above her. Fumbling, her fingers found the buttons of his fly, and quickly opened them. Above her, he tore at his webbing and swore; someone laughed in the background; he got the pack and kit free of his body, and she pulled his pants down, leaving his thin, solid cock jutting out from the thick bush of hair at the base of his belly. She tugged him and he fell bodily down on top of her.

'Oof!' *It's never like it is in the movies, is it?*

For a second, the sheer physical awkwardness of it put her off. Then she felt him covering her, the smoothness of his belly, the hairiness of his legs and chest, and the prodding head of his purple circumcised cock.

'You going to give me a blow job?' he breathed hopefully, a few inches away from her face. He smelled of the open air and of sweat; and she buried her face against his shoulder and inhaled before she answered.

'Maybe later. Depends how good a fuck you give me.'

'That's telling him, miss!' the Afro-Caribbean man yelled.

'I'm not here to suck you lot off,' Fern said, with more confidence, despite the man's weight squashing her, 'I'm here to pull a train, and you guys are going to fuck me in turn till you turn blue!'

'Till *who* turns blue?' Johnson chuckled in his throat. His face above her was white and sweaty. His cock pushed against her thigh, and she reached down the length of his body to press it against her wet pussy hair.

'You aren't nothing but a dick!' Fern gasped. She fisted her hands in his uniform jacket, yanking his body closer to hers. The warmth of it made her hot. She writhed under him, her cleft growing warm and dissatisfied. Her hips thrust up against him without any thought from her. 'Fuck me, if you can!'

He shifted his weight on her, driving the breath from her body. His hand closed over hers, where she gripped his cock, and he used his hand to make hers slide up and down, up and down...

'Careful,' he winced. 'I ain't got the roll-neck pullover some of this lot have!'

Fern sprawled back, giggling. She opened her legs and wrapped them around his waist, feeling the leaf-bits clinging to her bare skin. She felt his hand at her cunt, fingers prising open her dripping lips.

'You're gagging for it!'

'*Damn* right!'

As his hips thrust against her, driving his slender cock up into her, she bit down on his shoulder, tasting sweat and dirt. Her own sweat blurred her vision. She clenched her inner muscles down on him.

He yelled, 'Oh God I'm gonna *come*—!'

His hips jerked up against her. She felt a hot flood of his seed inside her. He sank down, breathing in gasps, and she felt his heart hammering. Though she was nowhere near orgasm, she felt herself full and semi-satisfied.

'Move it, Johnson, move it!' the blonde woman's voice barked from somewhere above her. Her tone sounded half thick with desire and half about to burst into laughter. *She's right, the only way she can be here for this is to put herself in charge of it.* 'Beckman, you're next!'

Fern hitched herself up on her elbows. She grinned at Johnson as he rolled off her, his slick, limp penis flaccid on his thigh. With a rueful look at her, he got to his feet.

'Ain't that the problem,' he muttered. 'Men are single-shot, and women are fully automatic . . .'

'What – *ooof*!' Fern felt herself collapse back under a heavy male weight. She looked up into the Afro-Caribbean soldier's face. He had stripped off his trousers and combat jacket, and he lay on her entirely naked except for a pair of the most unerotic pants she could ever have imagined.

'Beckman, is it?' She grinned. 'Just get rid of them, will you? I want to see if you live up to the stereotype.'

One of the other soldiers, his hand down the front of his trousers, called out cheerfully, 'You'll be lucky if you can find it!'

Fern snuffled back a giggle. *This isn't supposed to be funny!* But they're such a *nice* bunch of guys . . .

She lay back as Beckman reached down the long, smooth black length of himself, and discarded his white underwear. Naked, he was all smooth black surfaces, a little paler on his arms. The palms of his hands and the soles of his feet were honey-coloured; the rest of him black-brown velvet.

He didn't lie on top of her, but beside her. One of his large hands reached out and stroked her body from her shoulder to her breast, and her breast to her belly – her stomach fluttered with arousal. His fingers trailed past her pussy, tantalisingly not touching her, and then smoothed warmly down her thighs.

'I never was with a lady who didn't enjoy it,' he rumbled, smiling. As she reached for his hand, he caught hers. He lay, a lithe line of muscle, with broad shoulders and tapering torso, narrow hips and strong thighs. His groin was almost hairless. His cock jutted out, straining darkly, a bead of clear liquid at its uncircumcised tip.

Fern freed her hand and touched her fingers to his skin, tracing the line of the big vein underneath his cock. It shivered and jerked at her touch, and swelled even more; thick and juicy. She could feel herself running wet with her own juices as well as Johnson's cum.

'I'll enjoy it!' she promised, stuttering, 'I will – just fuck me!'

'Oh, you will . . .' he murmured. He rolled over on to her, taking his weight on his hands, and looked down at her for a moment, his bobbing dark cock between their bodies. Fern spread her thighs and lifted her legs. She saw her own flesh pale against his. He began to rub his hips up and down, teasing the entrance to her vagina with the head of his thick cock.

'Don't make me wait!' Fern wrapped her arms around his back and her legs around his waist, trying to pull herself up, as if she could impale herself on him. She felt the thick hot tip press into her lips, then move back; press and move back . . .

'Fuck me!' she yelled, and one of his arms went around her, crushing her to his thick chest. She felt his body move between her thighs, stretching her open.

Before she could speak again, she felt the tip of his cock pressed hard at the entrance to her cunt. He moved his other hand to her hip, his hand all but big enough to cover her, and his fingers dug into her flesh and pushed down as his hips thrust up. Wet and ready, she felt him begin to slip inside her. The thickness of him pushed her apart, stretching her, filling her, still pushing her open – *God, he's big!* – and she let her head fall back and her body go limp in his arms, conscious of nothing but being filled to the brim with hot, sweating, swollen flesh.

Gradually, slowly at first, he began to pump her. His hips ground her into the grass and leaves. She clung to him, rocked back and forth; and she felt him grow inside her – grow impossibly, until she was on the cusp between pleasure and pain, stuffed full of him, stuffed full of a thick, hard cock that thrust up and drew back, thrust up and drew back, banging her arse against the ground, body slamming her wide open, cock jamming up her, hard and thick, hard and thick—

As his hips slammed into her, lifting her clear off the ground, she took the whole length of him inside her and exploded into orgasm; her cunt throbbing, pulsing, searing with the electric pleasure of coming. The thick flesh that she enclosed grew hot – he strained – she felt him strain – and as he came, jetting hot come into her, filling her up until it spilled out between their sweat-glued bodies, she came again, every muscle relaxing, fire sweeping through her, coming until she lost all consciousness of what she was doing, where she was; only her thrashing body left in the throes of her orgasmic extreme.

It might have been minutes later that she tasted

water and became aware of the blonde woman holding a water-bottle to her lips. She drank, gratefully. Then she hitched herself up on her elbow again.

'You okay?' the woman said, her voice furry with arousal.

'Why don't you try me and find out?' Shakily, Fern reached out and took the woman's hand, and pressed it to her breast. Her skin was so sensitive that she shivered at the feeling of strong, warm fingers.

'No – are you *sure* you're okay?' The woman took her hand back, and felt Fern's forehead with the backs of her fingers.

'Sure. You don't think I'm going to stop now, do you?'

'Well . . .'

'Okay.' Fern swallowed. 'I do feel a bit shaky. It's not like the movies, is it? But – oh, one more! I got to do one more.' She grinned mischievously. 'There must be someone wants Beckman's sloppy seconds . . .'

'I don't think any of them think they can compete!'

When she raised her head, Fern couldn't keep from grinning again. She was sitting in the middle of a jerk-off circle. Each of the men – except Beckman, who lay on his back breathing in slowing gasps – had their cocks out of their pants and were pulling away.

'There's only one thing that can't compete with a man, and that's a woman – but I see what you mean about army discipline,' Fern said regretfully.

She heaved herself up to a sitting position. A certain shakiness told her she might do well to leave it at that. *But I'll never get another chance . . .*

'I tell you what we're going to do,' she said. 'You're going to do what it is you guys are doing . . . and when you're ready, you're going to give me your cum . . . all over me.'

118

It was the sort of thing she'd said in her fantasies, often. To say it out loud, and to men with their hard dicks in their hands . . .

And it is real. That's the difference. It is real.

Fern rolled up on to her knees. She stayed there, kneeling, her legs parted, one hand in her sopping groin. She let her gaze move from Johnson, whacking his thin cock again, to the other blond boy, pulling at his uncircumcised cock with a water-reddened clumsy hand; to the shaven-headed soldier who hadn't even bothered to take his webbing off, but sat with his thickening pale cock jutting out of his fly. As they pumped their hands, sliding on their smooth cock-skin, she pushed her fingers down into her strip of pussy hair, and down, further down, finding her swelling clitoris—

'I'll do that,' the blonde woman said. She lay down, rolling over on to her back with ease, and shifted herself until she lay underneath Fern's kneeling ass. Fern reached up and grabbed a low tree-branch as the woman's mouth closed over her pussy, and the strong, hot tongue flicked at her inner lips, the mouth of her cunt, the hood of her straining, swollen clitoris.

'Take this!' a rough male voice grunted. Hot semen spurted across her face. She gasped, hanging on to the tree-branch, feeling the corporal's tongue pressing deep into her cunt, flicking and sucking, probing between her inner walls, and another jet hit her, hot and salty; hit her in the face and trickled down, running over her breasts; another spurt, and another, and the woman's tongue left her crack and a small fist jammed up her as the tongue stuck itself right up her ass, and she lost her grip on the branch and hung, gripped between two men as she swayed, boneless, into a climactic explosion that seared through her cunt and lost her all control; she came and pissed, helplessly, over the other woman's fist, and then came again, shudderingly, shatteringly, as she had never come before.

'... I was lucky to find nice guys,' Fern said, sprawled back across the bed. Alix watched her face in the mirrors on the wardrobes, saw the girl's pupils dilated with remembered desire.

'A lot of people *are* nice.' Alix shrugged.

'It's just – these are fantasies I've had for a long time. *Doing* them is ... something else. For one thing, I got sore!'

Alix found her fingertips tracing the moulded lines of the black dildo. She absently clicked the switch on, off, on, off ... 'Of course, there *are* shitheads out there, so we need to be careful ...'

'You going to do anything with that, or are you just running my battery down?'

Alix sat up on the bed. She looked down at the naked back in front of her and Fern's pointy chin resting on her arms. She reached across and traced the vibrating head of the dildo across Fern's tight, pert buttocks, watching the flesh quiver. She pictured the younger girl spreadeagled on the forest floor, taking each man of a squad up her ...

'Oh, I expect I might do *something* to run the battery down,' Alix remarked, innocently. 'Or you might. Do you want to play the corporal this time?'

Chapter Nine

THE LAWNS SURROUNDING THE college buildings were bright with hundreds of students in summer dresses or sports kit; splotches of colour against the green of the grass. Some sat reading textbooks. Some just sprawled on the turf, young bodies exposed to the sun.

The gravel on the walkway crunched under Alix's sandals as she walked between Fern Barrie and Professor Mayhew.

'And do you find your sexual response is deepening?' Vivienne Mayhew asked.

Alix caught Fern's eye. The younger woman grinned.

'You could say that,' Alix agreed cautiously. 'The trouble is . . .'

'This is trouble?' Fern Barrie murmured under her breath.

Alix saw Vivienne Mayhew glance up at the cloudless sky. She steered them off the path, and under the pleached alley that ran around the college's formal gardens. Now, in this hot afternoon, it was a green tunnel of light, only kept from being stifling by the slight movement of a breeze along it.

Alix looked up at the ever-shifting vine leaves. She brushed her hair back from her sweating face.

'It's wonderful. *But*. The trouble is,' Alix said, 'it isn't fantasy, it's real life, and . . . I don't know. You have to clear up after everything. The people are still *there* when you've finished. It doesn't all magically vanish. I'm almost feeling it's more trouble than it's worth!'

Fern snuffled a giggle, bouncing to sit on one of the garden benches. She was wearing a crop-top that stretched tightly across her rounded breasts and a microskirt that barely covered her smooth thighs, and when she put her bare foot up on the edge of the bench, Alix caught a glimpse of her little white cotton panties. A flush of heat went through her.

'And is it?' Vivienne Mayhew said, seating herself beside Fern. 'More trouble than it's worth?'

'Oh . . .' Alix lifted one shoulder in a shrug. A smile of satisfaction tugged at her mouth. '*No*. But sometimes it can feel like it, I guess; you know what it's like – well, no, you don't know; you're not doing this—'

'I am.'

Fern Barrie put her foot down on the path again and sat up. If she were a cat, Alix thought, the younger woman's ears would have been pricking up.

'*You* are?' Fern said, incredulous.

'I wouldn't ask any of my students to do anything I won't do myself.'

'But you're old—!'

Alix caught Vivienne's eye and whooped. The forty-something academic was in a dark copper-and-bronze-printed dress, close-fitting at the bodice, where her deep-shadowed cleavage showed, and flaring out into a full skirt. The colours should not have worked as a summer dress, but in that light filmy material, and with her dark hair and her perfect gypsy complexion, it did. Splendidly.

'Not old,' Fern Barrie added hastily. 'Not old, you know what I mean, just not my age, not Alix's age – oh, *shit*!'

Professor Mayhew was grinning at her student's consternation, Alix saw. Sunlight through the green leaves glinted on the gold at her ears and the fine gold chains around her neck. A fine black-net triangular shawl, tied around her hips, emphasised her hour-glass figure, the black picked up again by the fine leather straps of her black sandals. Her hair, loose, caught a silver glint every so often, but was mostly a lush, dark, brunette cloud. Despite her youthful attitude, there was no mistaking her for a girl – she was all woman. A dark rose in full, sensual flower.

'What have you tried?' Alix asked.

It must have been apparent there was more than curiosity behind her question. Vivienne Mayhew nodded thoughtfully. 'It's difficult to know exactly what we're finding out, isn't it? I suppose there's no reason that we shouldn't pool our experience. Mine was a few days ago . . .'

Vivienne Mayhew looked at the e-mail she had been composing on her PC monitor. She read it through again. The power of words, she thought to herself.

Have I said this the way I want to? Will it make them do as I ask?

She looked down at her hands on the keyboard. The flawless olive skin of her fingers set off the clear nail varnish and her discreet gold rings. They were not the hands of a girl.

But they were shaking.

Sighing, dry-mouthed, she read through the e-mail for the third or fourth time:

Alan,
I know it's been a while since we've spoken. I expect we have some things to work through. Perhaps we could meet up for lunch and resolve some of our hostility?

You may wish to bring Robin with you – as ever, he will have much to contribute.

Vivienne

She moved her hand to the mouse. Innocuous words, as befitting a message that could theoretically be read by thousands of people, and perhaps stored by them, and that could always be traced back to her.

If I had Alix Neville's talents at concealing my e-address, I'd put it all more bluntly, she thought. She hit Send. Over the modem's tweedles and burbles, she heard herself chuckle.

'Dear God, suppose he *does* come to lunch? Will anything happen?'

It will if you want it to.

'Yes,' she murmured aloud again, answering that inner voice. 'It will, won't it? All those things I've been writing down . . .'

There was nothing here in the office; she could pick up her bag and lock the room and happily leave it. At home, it was different. At home, in a combination-lock fire safe, were half a dozen reporter's thick notebooks, filled with her large, elegant scrawl. Handwritten because she didn't want to put anything on a modem-accessible PC or find anything lurking on a hard disk that she thought had been erased.

Her low-heeled shoes tapped along the college's

corridors. She exchanged a word or two with students on the way. Outside, under a thunder-purple sky, she estimated the chance of rain, and called for a taxi rather than risking the walk to the station. Before they were within two miles of her flat, forked lightning stabbed the high-rise-studded horizon. She felt the fine, faint hairs on her arms standing up with the tingle of electricity in the air.

And at home, despite the rumbling of thunder down towards the London estuary, she switched on her own PC and checked her mail. *There won't be anything yet*, she thought, chiding herself for her impatience. *Alan has a life apart from me now.*

A few drops of rain had spattered her as she ran indoors from the taxi. She rubbed her hand through her masses of hair now, shaking away the droplets. Dark rain-blobs moistened her silk tabard-top and gypsy skirt. She hooked her shoes off and wriggled her bare toes in the luxurious carpet.

I must have been on quite some ego-trip while I was decorating this place, she reflected, glancing round at the terracotta walls, the high bookshelves, and the space she'd left to display her own degree certificates, and copies of *Hidden Pleasure* and her other books. *Wasn't that just after I got over Alan making me feel rather smaller than a woodlouse? Compensation, obviously. I could put them away again now.*

She muttered a curse under her breath and hit Connect again. The modem whistled and screeched.

She saw that she was receiving mail, and her heart all but stopped.

With clumsy fingers, she brought up the message.

My dear Vivienne,
Curious that you should write when you've been

so much in my thoughts recently. The repeat of your series on television gives Robin and me a great deal to talk about. Certainly we should have lunch.

Why don't you drive up to the old house today? Call ahead and let me know when you're arriving: we'll arrange a welcome for you.

Alan

Vivienne sank down into the chair in front of her desk. For a long time, she sat with her elbows on the desk, and her lips resting against her linked fingers, staring at the screen.

Has he realised. . . ? He mentions the programme. It could read that way. Or – what I wrote was very ambiguous. Is he trying to sound me out in turn?

She nipped her lush lower lip between her teeth for a moment, frowning. The tiny pain concentrated her attention. She let the abused flesh go, and licked her lips. Then she picked up the phone and dialled.

'Alan?'

'Vivienne . . . you got my e-mail, then?'

'Oh yes.' She paused. 'I was wondering how correct I might be in reading between the lines.'

There was a silence on the other end of the phone. Then his rumbling voice murmured, 'As was I . . . about the "hostility" . . .'

Another pause.

His voice came down the phone-line again. 'Would that be your hostility towards me, or mine to you?'

'Oh, both. And both of us towards Robin.'

'*Both* of us?'

'I feel hostile towards the man who broke up my first marriage,' Vivienne said, gazing at the rain-spotted window, not really seeing the forked lightning over the

City. 'You'd expect that, wouldn't you? But I think you feel hostile towards him too, from time to time, for the same reason. You were ... comfortable ... here. He made you face up to your other desires.'

Alan's voice was warmly intimate in her ear. 'I have many desires, but you're still included in them, you know that. I always wished we could have remained ...'

His voice trailed off. Vivienne's mouth quirked. *Why can't you be as honest as my students are with each other?* 'You mean you wish we'd remained friends who sleep with each other?'

There was a startled pause on the other end of the line.

'Well,' he said. 'Yes.'

'I haven't been short of company since we divorced. In fact, sometimes I still wear my wedding ring, because it cuts down on the number of men who proposition me. I just have the ones who appeal to me ...' She felt happiness welling up inside her as she spoke. *This* is *the right thing to do!* 'My life has been much happier, and much freer since you left me for Robin. Alan, I'd like to wipe out the last of the resentment I feel, and for us to be friends – if not close friends. But that will require something from you.'

'What's that?'

Something in his tone – a thickness, however well-disguised – made her smile to herself. *We always did know how each other's minds worked. He's way ahead of me here.*

'Sex can be the best way to work through hostility,' she said out loud. 'That's why "fuck" is aggressive. You let me come to the house, and I'll make my arrangements for working through my feelings. All that has to happen is – you, and Robin, are to do everything I tell you to.'

127

'I don't know if I—'

'You mean, you don't know if *Robin* wants to. Talk to him. I'll drive up. If you're at home when I get there – then you've agreed. If you've gone out – we'll never mention this again.'

She put the phone down with a click, her hand shuddering as she took two attempts to settle it. Not letting herself think, she changed, found her car keys, launched herself out into the traffic, and drove north of London into the Home Counties on autopilot. For all the rain, spray and rat-runs to avoid gridlock, she was not mentally present – was in a strange state of mind between anticipation and fear.

And if it doesn't work . . .

'If it doesn't work out the way it does in my fantasies – there's a very good reason we're divorced. I don't *have* to see him again, ever!'

His car was standing in the farmhouse drive.

She drew her car up beside it, not caring that she splashed it with mud. Here the rain had been over for a time, and the puddles reflected back glowing sunlight. The converted farmhouse stood, windows blank, against the green expanse of the woodland beyond. The only other buildings in sight were two falling-down barns: bought for conversion but, like so many other joint plans, never brought to fruition.

What do I do if Alan's here but not Robin?

Well . . . it won't be like the fantasy. But will it be okay?

'Let's see, shall we?' she said, unlocking the car door and sliding out. The scent of wet grass filled her nostrils. She could hear birds singing, a dog barking a long way off and the distant hum of a jet. Her steps sounded unnaturally loud as she took her bag from the car and walked up the concrete slipway to the back door of the farm. The door opened as she got there.

Her first thought was, *Why do men just get more distinguished as they get older!*

His black hair had a few silver streaks at the temples. For the rest, he was the same lean, broad-shouldered man she'd met in Chicago on a book-tour, thinking nothing of it at first except for the coincidence of their both being from the UK and meeting in the States. His belly looked a little soft under the worn blue check shirt, but his hips were still tight and neat in his blue denim jeans.

Another face appeared in the doorway behind Alan. Beautiful in a boyish but very masculine way, with bright eyes behind dark lashes and bottle-blond cropped hair – he looked a baby-faced twenty-five, not well over thirty. She nodded acknowledgement of him. 'Robin.'

'We're ready!' he blurted.

She looked away from him, and back towards Alan. 'Tie him up,' she said.

She had a length of clothes line in her bag. Her palm sweating, she held the rope out. In mundane daylight, in the open air ... surely they would laugh, both of them, and she would storm back to the car and feel ten times a fool?

The black-haired man reached out and took the rope. One hand on his lover's shoulder turned the younger man around. Vivienne watched as the tanned, broad fingers of her ex-husband knotted the rope around the younger man's wrists. She began to feel a warmth in her groin.

'Shall we take him indoors?' Alan murmured.

Vivienne looked him up and down, taking her time. At last she said, 'There is no "we". I didn't tell you you could speak, did I?'

'No, but—'

'That just adds to the scorecard, Alan. And it's getting very long.' She held his gaze until his eyelids flickered down over his green eyes, and he couldn't look her in the face. 'This is the boy you left me for. This is the boy who took you out of your comfortable home. I think he's been spoiled in comfort for much too long, don't you?'

Robin turned his head, trying to look over his shoulder at her. His bright gaze was calm, but she could see sweat on his forehead. She moved a step or two closer, looking him up and down in much the same way.

She caught a glimpse of herself in the glass panel of the back door: the above-the-knee black skirt, the business jacket, the tumbles of brown-black hair bound up on the back of her head. There was no smile on her face; it made her look official, authoritarian, severe.

'Let him earn his keep,' she said dismissively. 'Have him suck you off.'

A faint pink flush coloured Alan's well-fed features. He opened his mouth to speak, closed it again, and looked to her as if for permission. She nodded. He said, 'Where...?'

'There.' She pointed, almost at random, down the drive. The road that went past the house was not well frequented, but there was a chance someone might see ... She felt the heat in her thighs, brushing together, as they walked a few steps down the drive. She stopped, standing on the concrete path. 'Here.'

'But—'

'Here!'

Alan pushed the younger man forward. Robin stumbled, losing his balance with his hands tied behind his back. He fell forward, coming down hard on both knees – into the mud at the side of the drive. The rich brown slurry splashed his pale chinos and black T-shirt, and a slanting gob of it plastered itself across his face. He blinked and blew out his lips. '*Al*an—'

'Shut up,' Vivienne said coolly. 'Turn round. You're going to suck my husband off, right here, where anybody can see you on your knees to him.'

The warmth in her vagina became heat. She felt the slickness of her skin as she moved slightly where she stood. The impulse to cup her own breast and squeeze it was almost irresistible, and she had to fight to keep from pressing her fingers against the front of her skirt.

'Do it!' she snapped.

His head hanging down, the young blond man shuffled awkwardly around on his knees in the mud. He made to reach up towards the older man, tugging his tied hands apart behind his back, but Vivienne stopped him with a gesture.

'You're a clever boy,' she said caressingly. 'You'll think of something.'

His blue eyes momentarily met hers. Resentment and lust seemed mixed in his expression. He stretched up, his hands still bound before him, and nuzzled at Alan's fly. Alan gasped, and put his own hands behind his back. Vivienne watched as Robin carefully turned his head and caught the zip between his teeth, tugging at it.

She imagined the heat of his moist breath on her own groin and groaned under her breath. Almost as if it was her own, she felt Alan's cock swell in his jeans. She felt the urge to reach between his legs and cup his scrotum and squeeze his balls—

Not yet. Not yet!

The bulge in Alan's pants grew bigger, stiffer. The younger man snorted, breathing harshly through his nose. The zip wouldn't come down, no matter how he worried at it with his teeth. Vivienne dropped her gaze to his mud-spattered chinos, and saw that he too was swelling in his pants.

'Can't you do *anything* right?' she whispered scornfully. She had the satisfaction of seeing him flinch at her spite.

But I don't want to destroy him . . . either of them. What I told Alan was true – this is a way to work through things.

'Alan, help him.'

The big black-haired man let out his breath in a gasp. His face was bright red. He brought his hands round to his fly, wrenching at the zip. Robin leaned back upright, panting, his eyes fixed on the older man's crotch. With a muttered obscenity, Alan yanked his jeans open and dropped them, and they fell to his knees. He slipped his hands under the waistband of his boxer shorts and slid them down, his pale, thick cock jutting out into the cool, rain-soaked air.

Vivienne felt her lips curving into a smile. *I'd forgotten his white hairy legs. And now anyone could see them...*

'Now suck him off,' she said, her voice dry. She pressed her arms into her body, feeling the sides of her breasts tender and aroused. Robin leaned forward where he knelt, opening his mouth and taking the head of Alan's penis inside. Vivienne saw him tighten his lips and then slide his mouth up and down the shaft. The angle of Alan's erection altered, straining towards the sky.

Surreptitiously, she brought her bag around in front of her and held it with one hand. Her other hand slid under it, her fingers pressing the material of her skirt against her groin. She felt the throbbing swell of her clit under her fingers and rotated her pelvis minutely as she stood staring at how Alan's thick cock stuffed the young man's mouth.

'Oh, I can't hang on—!' Alan threw one arm out, grabbing hold of her shoulder. She felt his fingers dig in, hard, and his hips jutted forward, and he came in the younger man's mouth, fully, copiously, cum filling Robin's mouth, leaking out between his lips. He dropped both hands down and pressed the young blond man's face into his groin. 'Oh *God*!'

Vivienne braced her feet apart on the ground, looked at the mud-covered man on his knees, cum running down his face, and pressed her fingers hard into her clitoris. A shiver of pleasure ran through her body.

Alan said hoarsely, 'Now—'

'Now *you*,' she interrupted. She looked around. She pointed. 'Over there.'

There was a heap of builders' materials, left when the conversion of the barns failed to happen. Most of it was covered in tarpaulin, weighted down with chunks of concrete. One bench stood exposed to wind and weather. Beyond it was a barrel.

Alan stumbled beside her, hauling up his jeans and panting. She reached out and grabbed the back of his waistband, steering him.

'What? I – *oof*!' he gasped, as the edge of the barrel hit him in the pit of his stomach.

'Get up on that.'

'But—'

'I didn't tell you to talk!'

The younger man squelched up to stand beside her. His face was flushed red. His nostrils expanded as he dragged in air, and he wiped his face roughly against his shoulder. His hands were still tied, but his humiliation was fading; he was starting to grin, she saw. He shot a glance at her, and she nodded and untied him.

The young man reached out and grabbed the seat of her husband's jeans, hoisting him up face forward over the barrel. Alan fell forward with a grunt. She walked round to stand in front of him. As he gazed at her, she reached into her bag and took out a rubber ball-gag.

'No, Vivienne—!'

'I keep telling you,' she murmured, 'you need to keep your mouth shut – and, in this case, your arse open. I'm going to watch while your fancy-boy fucks you up the arse. And you're not going to say a *thing*.'

She let her hands rest against the back of his head long enough for him to have objected. Not looking at her, he shifted himself further forward and opened his mouth, taking the rubber ball between his teeth. She reached down, stuffed it home, and buckled up the straps.

Stepping back, she regarded him for a minute. He lay face down over the barrel, his legs forced wide apart by its girth. She smiled. Taking the rope that had tied up the younger man, she crossed Alan's wrists at the small of his back and lashed them together.

'He has to annoy you sometimes,' she breathed at Robin. 'Now you have a chance to let him know how it feels to be on the receiving end . . .'

Slowly, the boy reached out and pulled Alan's jeans down, exposing his white arse to the air. Vivienne could see the erection he had in his chinos – a monstrously thick cock outlined against the thin, wet material. Suddenly he bent down and scooped up a handful of the glutinous mud. With his other hand, he parted Alan's buttocks, and then slapped the cold, liquid mass up his arse.

'Oh my God . . .' Vivienne almost came in her panties. She rummaged through the bag and handed Robin a tube of KY, and then straightened up as he undid his fly and anointed himself: all ten inches of thick, fat, red-purple cock. His hand closed round it, working the foreskin up and down. She staggered a couple of steps back, behind him, and fumbled her skirt up, pushing her fingers down the front of her knickers.

Her clitoris jutted against her fingers, lubricated by the juices flowing from her cunt. She slid her fingers down her labia, and then between them, into the searing heat of her cleft; rubbing at the inner walls. She straightened back up, keeping the pad of her middle finger on her clit, rotating it gently.

Shocks of pleasure began to go through her flesh. She gasped, biting at her lip, not wanting to yell out loud. In front of her, Robin tugged down his chinos and his white arse bobbed. She leaned her head, watching as he took his cock in his hand and rubbed it over Alan's buttocks. He slathered KY at the older man's puckered hole and then braced himself.

'You're going to get it!' Vivienne said aloud. 'It's him doing it, but it's me giving the orders, Alan – it's me fucking you right up your faggot ass!'

With that she dropped the bag, stepped forward, and pressed her groin up against Robin's bum. She heard him chuckle, then gasp. She clung, pressing her body tight against him, feeling him lift himself on his toes, and then suddenly thrust his cock right home.

There was a muffled strangled yell: Alan through the gag.

She gripped Robin's bare hips, grinding her pelvic bones against him, shoving him forward, pushing, thrusting, as if she could shaft Alan with the younger man's cock, as if she could make him impale himself helplessly on her, fucked until he yelled for mercy.

The younger man slumped forward.

Dazed, Vivienne slumped with him. She remained

prone for a second, finally realised Robin had come, and stood up. Her legs shook, her cunt was on fire; she groaned under her breath. *Oh God, I need to fuck!*

She shut her eyes, groaning again. When she opened them, it was to find Robin undoing Alan's gag and helping him down. The black-haired man clung to his lover's shoulder. She grinned, lips skinned back from her teeth, feral.

'What?' she said, as Alan said something for the second time. 'What was that?'

'I said, you're not the only one with hostility to work off!'

She put her hands out in half-hearted protest. Two male bodies closed in on her, Robin facing her, Alan at her back. She said weakly, 'You won't dare!'

His hot breath feathered her ear. 'Dare what, Viv?'

'Won't dare . . . fuck me front and back . . . cunt and arse . . .'

She felt hands at her thighs, yanking up her skirt. A foot between her ankles jerked her feet apart. She swayed, only to find herself supported between them, her hands on Robin's shoulders. Cold air rushed up her skirt as it was lifted, and she shivered as someone's hands yanked her panties down.

'Nancy-boys! Faggots!' She yelled every insult she had wanted to shout out loud in court. 'You can't fuck a woman; you wouldn't know what to do!'

The heat in her groin seared her, and she thrust her hips forward against the bottle-blond boy. As she did, feeling him against her bare skin, Alan's hands tilted her head back and she felt her mouth stuffed full of the rubber gag. Hands gripped her, hoisting her; she felt her feet leave the ground. She screamed into the gag, thrashing her legs.

A handful of cold KY was slapped up her arse.

Fingers probed her sopping wet hot cunt. She yelled her throat sore, screaming, knowing she could not be heard more than a yard away; felt them lift and thrust—

Two cocks filled her. Robin's monster cock stuffed up her fanny; Alan's more slender, longer cock filling her arse. For a second she clung, jammed between their bodies, and then they began to thrust again. The solid bulk of their hard cocks filled her, ramming in, ramming up; in and out, in and out; her muscles loosening, her cunt juice running down her thighs, her head falling back on Alan's shoulder, her body jolted up, up, *up*—

Simultaneously a massive hot jet of come squirted up her arse and a salty hot fountain flooded her cunt. Her body exploded in waves of sensation, her throat yelling, her hips jerking, fire searing through her, convulsing her, losing all control as she came and came and came.

'... That was one of the best orgasms in my life.' Vivienne Mayhew looked up from where she sat on the bench. 'But, do you know what? I don't think I can write it up for the project.'

Alix grinned at her.

'Of course you can,' she said. 'Anonymously!'

Chapter Ten

'WE'RE IN TROUBLE!' Vivienne Mayhew snapped.

She did not do it particularly quietly. Other heads looked up in the library. Alix sat suddenly upright, spilling the books across her carrel, and swivelled round to face the older woman.

'We are?' she said, dopey and bewildered.

'Oh, yes!' The Professor swung on her sandalled heel. As she walked off, she said without looking back, 'And I need you as a witness, Alix, please. *Now.*'

Languorous sunlight shone through the windows of Pardoe College's modern library. She had been closer to sleep than study ... a state in which fantasy moved quite naturally across her mind, and the closed carrels and the long polished tables took on the air of sensual, heat-soaked locations for orgasm ...

Alix blinked at the woman's departing back. Vivienne's unbound curls of black-brown hair flicked with the sharpness of her steps, tapping away over the polished wooden floor towards the library doors.

She said *what*? We're what? Who's *we*?

Alix stood up. She swept the books into a rough heap and left a pen and pad on top: the recognised sign of a student who would return to them at some point.

Grabbing up her bum-bag, she walked swiftly after Vivienne Mayhew.

The library doors hissed closed behind her. The dark-haired older woman was waiting on the landing, in the glass-windowed stairwell. She paced back and forth. As Alix came up, she lifted a scowling face.

'Alix—' The scowl relaxed into a rueful expression. The harsh lines around her eyes and mouth faded to faint marks. She softened, visibly. 'I'm sorry, that was rude. But this makes me so *cross* – look!'

She pointed with one tanned hand to the floor-length windows. Her gold rings caught the sun, glimmering. Alix approached the glass. She looked out and down. This part of the library overlooked the front of the college and the main road that ran past it. For a second, Alix was at a loss. *What am I looking for?*

'Oh shit!' she exclaimed. 'Is that about you – about us?'

A small group of people occupied the pavement at the college gates. They were walking in a circle that took in the exit road, and some of them held posters on boards. Here on the first floor, Alix could get a clear enough look to read the lettering on some as they came round to face her.

STOP EXPLOITING WOMEN!
NO SEX-SLAVES IN COLLEGE!
MAYHEW OUT OUT OUT

'Oh my Gawd ...' Alix said under her breath. 'Professor Mayhew, who are they? What sort of nutters ...'

Vivienne Mayhew stepped closer to her. She stood at Alix's shoulder, an inch or so shorter even in the low heels. Her lush flowing hair smelled of musky perfume. The heat of the sun through the plate glass accentuated it. Alix found herself breathing in deeply.

'You want to know who they are?' the woman said bitterly. She pointed as another sign came around, held by a bare-armed redhead.

WOMEN AGAINST SEXUAL OPPRESSION OF WOMEN!

'They're feminists,' Vivienne Mayhew said. 'After all I've done—! *I'm* a feminist!'

Alix squinted, making out the parade more clearly. Two black women, one white, one who looked Korean or perhaps Japanese; another white woman; a black person who might be male or female, with close-cropped hair; another man . . .

'What are they doing here? How did they get to know about the project anyway?'

'I don't know!' Vivienne Mayhew protested. She put her elegant hands on her hips. It was a very determined stance, and it didn't quite go, Alix thought, with the gypsy-like black shawl around the Professor's hips, or the decidedly low-cut scarlet summer dress. *Or perhaps it does*, she thought.

'We'd better go down and talk to them, before the college authorities hear about it,' Vivienne added. Her forehead creased again. 'And at this particularly important stage of research . . .'

'Don't go down,' Alix said.

The older woman continued to look down at the scene outside. In profile, the line of her chin was deliciously soft. She had the air of an experienced woman in her prime.

'You think it's better to invite them in?' she said.

Alix nodded. 'Always better to be on home turf. I'll go give them the invite. Besides, they'll think it's a compliment if you see them in here – you're giving their protest legitimacy.' And at Vivienne Mayhew's stare, she added: 'I know all about office politics, don't forget.'

'So you do.' She smoothed dark hair back from her face, smiling at Alix as she did so. 'I tend to forget – you look younger than you are. I find myself assuming I'll have you here for the entire degree course, when I've really only got you for another month or six weeks.'

She's right! Damn, she's right . . .

A little more than a month, Alix thought, quickening her pace to trot down the stairs beside Vivienne Mayhew. *She's right – it's easy to think this will go on for ever. But it won't . . .*

The leader of the protest proved to be a lanky, tall woman in her late twenties. She walked with a relaxed ease in her body, her bare arms shining white in the strong sunlight. She had close-cropped hair dyed an explosive chemical red, and silver piercings in her ears, nose and lower lip. Her unsmiling, thin strong face had, Alix thought, powerful character behind it. Her eyes raked Alix while they talked, from bare shoulders to tanned legs; and Alix let her own gaze stray down over the woman's magnificent deep cleavage and neat hips in her black jeans.

Wow, she thought.

Negotiations over, the woman insisted on bringing a push-bike into the college park, pedalling in while finishing the cigarette she was smoking. Then, with a nod that gathered a demure-looking black woman in T-shirt and cut-offs into her company, she followed Alix up to Professor Mayhew's office.

'I think there are rather too many of us for my room,' Vivienne Mayhew said smoothly. 'Let's use the staff boardroom, shall we?' She opened a door further down the corridor and stood back. 'Ms – er—'

Alix moved back to let the redhead and the black woman pass by her.

The redhead said, in her husky hoarse voice. 'This isn't going to buy us off, you realise?'

The young black woman – she would be no older than Fern Barrie – added, 'We can be out there for as long as it takes for people to hear us. And we *will* be.'

The staff boardroom was nothing but a longer office, with the same high ceilings and row of sash windows down one side of the room that were features of most of the old part of the college. A long, dark, polished table ran down the middle of it, leaving hardly room for the rows of chairs. Both the redhead and her companion stood for a moment, and then the first woman sat down defiantly in the nearest chair and glared around her.

'Real old boys' club, isn't it?' she sneered. 'Professor Mayhew, I'm surprised you'd get involved with something like this – something that degrades women—'

Alix pulled out another chair, offering it to the black woman, who sat down. Looking around a little shyly, she said, 'I'm Jael.'

'Alix,' Alix said. 'I'm one of the Professor's students. Look, should I get us coffee—'

'You've even got your students acting as servants!' the red-headed woman said. Her eyes narrowed. They were a startling blue, Alix saw: enough of a chemical sapphire to be coloured contact lenses. Despite the sharpness of her, there was something paradoxically attractive about the woman.

Maybe I just like feisty women. Alix grinned to herself.

'Look,' she said, 'we can sit around arguing about who gets to be tea lady—'

'I'll do it,' Vivienne said firmly. 'I'll bring the kettle in from my room. Then we're going to sit down and talk this through. And I'll be interested to know how you came to hear about my work, Ms – er – what *is* your name?'

'Axley,' the redhead said.

'*"Axley"*?' Alix yelped. The woman glanced back over her shoulder at her.

'That's right. I'm Fran Axley.'

Sunlight illuminated her profile. There was no other resemblance, but Alix saw Jordan Axley's sharp-featured lines plain in this woman's face, hardly softened by femininity.

'Let me guess,' Vivienne Mayhew said grimly. 'You had a phone call from your – brother, would it be?'

The red hair dipped, catching the light as the woman nodded. Silver glinted from her earlobe, her lip and the side of her delicate nostril.

Vivienne Mayhew said, 'Isn't that Jordan Axley all over! He doesn't want to call major media attention to this college – after all, it's his job too. If he can persuade a pressure group to come and demonstrate here, though, and make the old dears on the board of governors nervous—'

'He didn't have to persuade us, once we heard what you were doing here!'

One phone call to, what, Leeds University? Alix wondered. *She's picked up a bit of the accent. And what did he tell her?*

'What did he tell you?' she asked.

It was Jael who spoke. 'We were surprised when Fran told us she had a brother working in this college . . .'

'He and I don't get on,' the red-headed woman added flatly. 'His view of lesbian separatists is—'

143

'Yes ...' Vivienne's dark lashes dipped over her gold-brown eyes for a moment. Alix saw her give the young woman a look of sudden, mischievous complicity. 'Yes, I *can* imagine.'

Fran Axley felt her back jeans pocket, and brought out a crumpled cigarette packet. She didn't take one out and light it, but instead sat tapping it on the polished wood of the long tabletop for a few seconds, staring at Vivienne Mayhew with a puzzled expression.

'He said you were a sexual reactionary who'd sold out to the heterosexual establishment,' she said abruptly. 'He said you wanted to make sure women only had hetero fantasies, and you were skewing your findings so that any potential dykes who read them would be put off lesbianism for life – "cured", he said!'

Alix thought she sounded suddenly much younger. Fran went on: 'He told me that you were giving your so-called "interpretations" of even the most clearly lesbian fantasies a heterosexual bias, trying to prove that the women who had them were really after men, not after other women at all. And you were dismissing any of your subjects who didn't fall into line with you as virtually certifiable perverts.'

'*What?*'

Alix snorted. It was the sheer outrage in Vivienne Mayhew's usually urbane voice that did it. She covered her mouth with her hand, not able to suppress a broad grin. When Jael and Fran Axley glared at her, Alix shrugged. 'Sorry. But the idea that – I'm one of the women on the project, you see. Vivienne thought I should talk to you, maybe reassure your group that ... well, but that's *so* ridiculous!'

'Is it?' The red-headed woman leaned back in the wooden chair, folding her arms across her chest. Her sinewy forearms flattened her breasts a little, pushing them up, and Alix looked hurriedly away from the scoop-front of her black T-shirt.

'It's not about exploiting anybody,' Alix protested. 'It's about finding out what you *really* want.'

The young black student, suddenly bitter, said, 'And how many of you "coincidentally" find out that what you want is a man?'

Vivienne Mayhew was busying herself with the coffee cups. She didn't look round. Alix, squinting in the dust-filled sunlight of the warm room, thought, *She's leaving it to me. As one of her students. Well, I guess that makes sense.*

'No, it's not like that,' Alix said. 'I've been doing this for several weeks, and . . .' Her voice trailed off, faced with Fran Axley's cold, sapphire-eyed stare. 'I'm not going to convince you, am I?'

Because your mind's already made up.

'I don't like my brother,' the skinny woman said. She wiped a pale hand across her face, suddenly; as if she could wipe away weariness. 'He's a right-wing berk, to tell you the truth. But even Jordie-boy isn't stupid enough to tell me something that's all smoke and mirrors. Even if it's just unconscious bias – the Professor's teaching you to be heterosexual. Whether *you* know it or not.'

A spark of annoyance flared in Alix's mind. She nipped her full lower lip between her teeth, trying to stop herself snapping back an insult. She took a deep breath. The smell of coffee wafted across the air, and the odours of dust, sunlight and female sweat, and Vivienne Mayhew's perfume.

'It strikes *me* Jordan Axley is capable of lying through his teeth!' Alix burst out. 'He thinks women fucking *anybody* is disgusting, whether it's men or other women! He'd just rather we didn't do it at all. *Or* think

145

about it. And I think he's told you just what you need to hear so that you'll cause a stink with the college authorities and this project will get stopped.'

Fran Axley slammed the cigarette packet flat on the table top. She got to her feet, lanky and powerful. 'Of course, you've swallowed the whole thing – the whole ideology. Just because this woman—' she gestured at Vivienne '—*is* a woman, that doesn't mean she's a feminist! Some of the worst oppression of women is by women. And when it's aimed at gay women—'

Alix stepped forward. She was conscious of the hissing of the steam from the kettle, and of Vivienne turning to look at them. The golden sunlight beamed through the windows, languourous as her daydreams in the library. She stood exactly the same height as Fran Axley. She reached out and put her hand on the other woman's arm, her golden tan seeming dark against the stark white of that skin. Fran's arm was warm under her fingertips.

Deliberately, she moved her hand up, and cupped it around the side of Fran Axley's breast. The globe of flesh swelled warmly into her hand. She leaned forward and put her lips on Fran's lips. They were soft and hot, and tasted slightly of cigarette smoke. She darted her tongue at the closed lips, jabbing until they opened. The tip of her tongue slid over the silver stud in the woman's lower lip. Her tongue slid in, and Alix opened her mouth wide and twined her tongue in the woman's hot mouth, tongue against tongue, breath hot and wet . . .

A surge of pleasure went through her groin. Her hand tightened on the heavy, soft breast lying against it. She felt the nipple stiffen against the heel of her hand. She realised she was pressing the woman back against the table's edge as her hot tongue probed every inch of Fran's mouth, their lips welded together.

With a gasp, she broke away from the kiss. Fran Axley stood stock-still, white arms hanging by her sides, her chest heaving. The breast in Alix's hand remained swollen. She felt the nipple erect through the thin cloth.

'Now do you believe me?' Alix gasped.

There was a moment of silence. Alix felt a breathtaking excitement, holding the woman's blue gaze.

Fran Axley smiled, suddenly, challengingly. 'Hey, anybody can *talk* a good fight.'

'That wasn't talk!'

'Yeah, but what would you do if I kissed you *back*, little girl?'

It was as if they were the only two people in the room. Alix did not smile. She stepped forward and put her hands either side of Fran's waist. Her torso was slender but solid, gym-healthy muscle under the skin rather than flab. This close, she could smell the scent of soap on the woman's pale skin. She saw that Fran had clean, very closely trimmed fingernails. The stud piercings in her ears caught the sun with dazzles of silver light that left swimming black marks across Alix's retinas.

Half dazzled, Alix shifted her grip and pulled the woman closer. She pressed her body against the body in front of her, belly to taut belly, breasts flattened against Fran's full round breasts, warm thighs pressing against thighs in tight denim. She felt her summer cotton dress flimsy, no barrier at all. Heat flushed her skin pink. Her sweat soaked through the fabric under her arms. She clearly felt the pressure of the buttons of the fly of Fran's jeans against her stomach and the heaving lift as Fran gasped in a breath.

Without giving herself time to think, letting her

body answer to impulse, she reached up and pulled the spaghetti-straps of the black T-shirt off the woman's shoulders. The T-shirt slid halfway down Fran's chest. Sunlight shone on the round, white globes of her breasts, and the enlarged big dark brown nipples. Alix dipped her head and took the right nipple into her mouth, sucking hard, feeling it stiffen and harden between her lips. She flicked her tongue in rapid butterfly-strokes across the very tip of the nipple, then pushed Fran's shoulders back and tried to cram as much of the hot flesh into her mouth as she could. Above her, she heard a high squeak of arousal, and the woman's knees sagged.

There were voices behind her – Vivienne and the woman Jael? – but Alix was oblivious. She took her mouth away, looking down at the flushed, saliva-smeared skin, the marks of her teeth red against the pale milky flesh. Her breath came hard in her throat.

'You don't – leave it there—' Fran said, half gasping, half growling.

Alix felt the woman move under her, shifting back and up. She realised that Fran was sitting up on the edge of the table. Her legs parted. Alix moved to stand between them. She felt strong, denim-clad thighs and calves lock around her waist, heels crossing behind the small of her back. Fran reached down and hauled her own T-shirt up and off.

With both hands, Alix cupped the full, white breasts, pushing them together. She bent forward and licked her tongue slowly, wetly, sensuously up the cleavage she had made. Her thumbs circled the dark nipples, pressing lightly, until Fran groaned and arched her back, thrusting her breasts up into the air, up towards Alix's mouth.

She dipped her head again, licking first one of Fran's

nipples, then the other. They sprang up, jutting in straining hardness. She put her face into the hot, sweaty cleft between the breasts, licking at salt sweat.

'Oh God!' Fran groaned. 'Do me! Oh God, yes!'

Alix saw her throw her arms back over her head in an ecstasy of desire. Lifting her head to follow the movement, she met Vivienne Mayhew's eyes. The older woman was standing on the far side of the table. Before Alix could blush or speak, Vivienne reached down and caught the redhead's outstretched wrists.

'Oh *yes* . . .' Fran breathed. Her eyes rolled shut. Alix felt Fran's ankles unhook behind her back.

Instantly, Alix leaned back and fumbled her way to the waistband of Fran's black jeans. She swore at the metal buttons, trying to undo them. At last the waistband popped open. Alix shoved her hand in, popping the fly buttons in quick succession. She felt hot, sweaty heat, and no other cloth.

Leaning back, she seized the denim at Fran's hips and pulled. The red-headed woman shifted in response, momentarily lifting her hips. Alix yanked her jeans down to her knees. Under them, Fran was naked: she wore no knickers. Her tuft of pubic hair, shaved into a stripe, was dyed a chrome chemical gold, stark against her milk-white belly and hips.

'Oh yeah . . .' Alix said, almost to herself. Her head swam. She found herself moving her thighs together, as if she could relieve the desire to come in her panties. Fran's skin felt soft under her hands: warm and fuckable. She fell forward and seized Fran's skinny body, pressing her small round breasts into the woman's groin. The warmth and smell of the flesh made her dizzy with wanting.

Sweatily, she slid down, until she was half-kneeling. She put her hands on Fran's hips, dipped her head and drew her tongue up the swelling flushed labia exposed to her view. Fran's whole body jerked, bare arse lifting off the polished table. Where Vivienne held her wrists, Fran's hands made fists.

Again, Alix dipped her head. She put her lips carefully on the hood of Fran's clitoris, teasing it with butterfly kisses, licking with the very tip of her hot tongue. Juices smeared her mouth, Fran's crotch, Fran's thighs and her breasts where she pressed them against Fran's thighs.

'Don't make me wait . . . ohhh!' Fran's voice trailed off.

Alix dipped first one shoulder then the other, hooking Fran's knees over her. The woman was laid out on the table now, hips lifted, cunt entirely exposed to Alix's gaze. Alix's hands dug into the woman's lean thighs.

Oh God, I wish I had a free hand!

She put her face in Fran's cunt, rubbing herself in the hot juices, smelling her, tasting her. She felt her own nipples hard as rocks under her dress. Her groin throbbed, fiery with unsatisfied desire.

A cool hand pulled up the back of her skirt and pulled down her panties.

Gasping, startled, Alix twisted to look over her shoulder.

'Hey, white girl.' Jael gave her a slow, sensual smile.

The Afro-Caribbean woman reached up to the back of her spaghetti-strap red T-shirt and stripped it forward over her head and off. She had already unzipped her denim cut-offs. Now she stepped out of them and stood naked.

Alix gaped, looking at her. Smooth dark flesh confronted her, shining in the sun. Over the curve of muscle of her arms, and over her collarbones, Jael was rich brown; fading to darker brown-black over her torso and belly. Plum-dark nipples perked as the air hit them. In the paler crease of her groin, Alix saw the beginning of tiny black curls; and as she moved her legs to stand boldly upright, Alix saw the mass of black hair on her mound of Venus. A glint of wetness quivered on the edges of the curls between her lips.

The black woman reached up and pulled the ribbon from her masses of hair, letting it spring free. Then she sank out of sight, kneeling. Alix felt her thighs held and opened. Her legs nearly giving way, she submitted to the pressure.

A hot, slow tongue lapped at her arse, her lips, her inner lips . . . she writhed, trying to get her clit into that honey mouth, and heard Jael chuckle teasingly.

'You get back to what you were doing to my girl,' Jael's voice said.

Spread-legged, Alix balanced above the spreadeagled Fran Axley. The red-headed woman had her head back now. Vivienne still pinioned her wrists, but the older woman had leaned forward. Her creamy breasts bulged out of the bodice of her dress. As Fran nipped the material between her teeth and delicately pulled, one of Vivienne's breasts popped out. The younger woman lifted her head and put her lips around Vivienne Mayhew's nipple.

Slow, lapping: a tongue caressed her labia, and Alix all but fell across the tabletop. Lips closed over the hood of her clit, gently sucking. She put her head down into Fran's groin, the woman's skin hot with sweat under her palms, and licked at her clit, heavy in its full, expansive hood. Under her lips, it jutted up hard.

'Oh *God*!' Fran's hips arched. Her body bucked, held up in the air for a second only by Vivienne's grip on her wrists, and her knees over Alix's shoulders. Alix held on, her face deep in the convulsing flesh, hot juices flooding over her tongue and mouth and cheeks. As Fran came she wrenched herself free – Alix felt the woman's legs sliding down off her shoulders, down her arms, and she was pushed back, up, her balance almost gone.

Chill air struck her flushed, dripping face.

Thrust almost upright, Alix felt three fingers slide into her cunt from behind. She stood stock-still. The deliciously thick obstruction slid in, and out . . . in, and out . . .

'Do me!' she yelled. 'Don't make me wait, oh God, don't make me wait!'

One soft strong arm encircled her hips and belly. The fingers slid out. What nudged at her labia then was not a finger, but something broader, more solid – the knuckles of a fist. Alix felt herself opening up like a flower, and the black woman's fist slid into her, inside her, pumping now, until her knees gave way.

Arms caught her as she half-fell. Fran Axley's white arms, strong and capable, holding her while a ring-pierced lip sucked her ear lobes, her nipples . . .

In and out, in and out: the black woman kneeling behind her pumping faster and faster, controlling her every sensation, until Alix could hold it no longer. She let go completely, held up by the two women, a fist jammed straight up her cunt, the friction teasing, forcing, thrusting; until she came explosively, ecstatically, flailing in their arms, her back arching, her feet off the floor.

No sound in the big room but the sobbing of breath. Heaving, gasping, gradually slowing.

'We ain't done yet,' Fran Axley said, her hoarse voice recovering. She rolled over on the table, kicking off her jeans and throwing aside her T-shirt so that she was white and naked. A sprinkle of freckles flecked her back, palest gold on milk. She reached forward to Vivienne Mayhew.

With a quick movement of her arms, Jael stripped her dress off over her head. Her dark eyes gleamed at Alix. She smiled in the sunlight, and climbed on to the long table, presenting Alix with a wide ass in a white silk thong.

Her pulse hammered in her throat. Alix climbed on top of the table. Kneeling behind Jael, she saw the woman's pendulous breasts hanging down, her body reflected in the polished surface. Over the Afro-Caribbean woman's shoulder, her own face was reflected, pale in the dark wood. *Oh, I do love to watch!*

Alix sat back on her heels. In front of her, Jael's ass jutted up into the air. Smooth, perfect, dark buttocks shone in the sun. Between them, the black-brown crease of her butt led down to her cunt, and plum-dark outer lips. Alix reached out with shaking fingers and carefully pulled Jael's panties aside. The ripe, pink inner cunt flushed invitingly, glistening with female cum-fluid. She slid her fingers lightly over the surface, and Jael groaned, eyes shut, dark skin flushing darker.

Further up the table, Fran's red hair was hidden, her head up Vivienne's skirt. The brunette lay with her knees up, rucking her scarlet skirts up to her hips. Her features were heavy with lust, flushed, and her dark eyes half-lidded.

'Oh,' Jael moaned, almost under her breath. 'Oh. Ohh . . .'

Alix dipped her middle finger into the hot wetness before her. She felt the inner walls of the woman's cunt clenching against her finger. Slowly, she began to slide it in and out, increasing the pressure, increasing the speed. Jael let her head fall down on to her arms, arse jutting up into the air. Alix, one hand thrusting into the swollen, hot folds of her sex, put her other hand down between her own thighs. She rubbed at her clit in the same rhythm with which she thrust into the black woman.

At last Jael's tight little cunt opened to her. She clenched three fingers thick and thrust them in, frigging as hard and as rapidly as she could. The woman began to cry out, gasping, sweat running down her dark back and breasts, her face twisting. Her shoulders rose, her neck arching. She breathed so hard and rapidly that her ribs showed under her brown skin. Alix thrust into Jael, rubbed herself; feeling her own clit harden again, swell, so sensitive that the merest touch was almost pain.

'Oh *yeah*!' the black woman screamed. 'Oh, shit, *yes*!'

Her thick, agonised, ecstatic tone did it: Alix's hips thrust forward of their own accord and she rubbed hard against her clit, and the feeling gathered in the deepest walls of her cunt and swept outwards, convulsing her, throbbing through her, searing pleasure; and she rubbed again, collapsing forward over Jael's prone body as she came again and again.

Rhythmic grunts came from further up the table. Alix lifted her head to see Fran Axley sprawled face down on the polished boardroom table. Vivienne sat on the small of Fran's back, facing Fran's feet, her skirt hiked up around her waist, her stocking tops and suspenders exposed. As Alix watched, she bent forward and put her face between Fran's thighs, sucking and licking. Alix strained to see, but Vivienne's skirts rustled down, hiding her ass.

Fran's body leaped in the older woman's grasp, her

open palm beating against the table top. Her eyes screwed tight shut. Her mouth fell open. She gasped, breathing as hard as if she was running a marathon; suddenly made fists of her hands, and jerked so hard that she threw Vivienne upright on her.

'Ohhhh YES!' Fran yelled hoarsely. She sprawled face down again, her chest heaving.

The scent of sweat and perfume, female bodies and cum-juice, drifted on the sunny air. Alix found herself lying beside Jael, too exhausted even to get off the table.

She smiled and slid a finger down Jael's side to her waist, and up the flaring lift of her brown hips and down and over her thigh. Jael's skin felt incredibly soft to the touch. Where her palms now opened, she was a yellow-brown colour, soft and honeyed. The soles of her feet were pale, too. Alix touched her again, putting all her fingers on Jael's pussy hair, with a pulse of pleasure in her groin.

'Are we done yet?' Alix grinned at Jael. Then her gaze went beyond the woman's midnight hair, to Vivienne. She felt her belly tighten. *If we're swapping round—*

Jael murmured, 'I don't think so—'

'We're done,' Vivienne said. Her voice was brisk, but she spoke in gasps.

Alix continued to gaze along the table. Still clothed, Professor Vivienne Mayhew sat astride a naked redhead, looking at her delicate gold ladies' wristwatch.

'We *are* done,' Vivienne said. 'This room was only free for an hour!'

There was a concerted scramble up and into clothes. Alix, recovering her knickers from under the table, and suddenly feeling disappointed, thought, *If we'd carried on, would it have been my turn with Vivienne? Because she is some woman . . .*

'Well,' Jael's soft voice said, 'I'm convinced.'

All three of them looked at her. Fran Axley was the first one to snort a laugh: a harsh sound like a kitten's sneeze, that changed into a full-blown bellow of laughter.

'Oh, yeah,' she said, after she wiped her eyes. 'I think Professor Mayhew can be cleared of having an oppressive agenda, all right.'

Alix chuckled.

Fran nodded to her. 'No more pavement demos,' she added. 'We'll be on our way. Oh, and before I go, I'm going to have a word with my brother . . .'

Occupied with writing up her experiences in the Professor's office, Alix couldn't hear what Fran said to Jordan Axley, but she heard the tone, ringing in scorn down the corridors of the college staff block; and after Fran had gone, Jordan Axley's office remained quiet for a long time.

Chapter Eleven

SOME DAYS LATER, ALIX walked across the college car park, a brown envelope held tightly in one hand. She smiled to herself as she felt the limpid summer air on her bare arms and legs, barely stirring the mass of silver-blonde hair that she wore down around her shoulders. *If this one works . . . I sure got hot* writing *it!*

The roads being crowded now with tourists on their way to the *Cutty Sark* at Greenwich, it had taken her far too long to drive in to college. She glanced at her watch, looked up at the college windows; calculating the time necessary to run up to Vivienne Mayhew's office, and if she could then make it unnoticed into the lecture room . . .

'Hey, Alix!' Fern loped over from the row of bikes. Her leathers were undone to the waist, showing a skimpy white crop-top soaking with sweat between her breasts. 'Hey, you got time for the refectory?'

'No, I have to drop this in to Vivienne, then dash.' Alix shaded her eyes with one tanned hand. The sun dazzled her, bouncing back off the glass college doors. She recognised the way one of the approaching figures carried herself, despite that. 'Ah. There she is.'

A hard white sky hammered down heat. Even the

elegant Vivienne seemed to have succumbed to it, Alix saw. A sweat-soaked tendril of brown-black hair plastered the older woman's forehead.

'Professor—'

'That is *it*!' Vivienne Mayhew proclaimed. 'Fern, Alix. This is the last straw! That man – oh, I swear I'm going to *strangle* him!'

Fern Barrie caught Alix's eye. The younger girl grinned, under her newly washed spiky hair. She tongued the piercing in her lower lip. 'Let me guess,' she said. 'Professor Axley again?'

'It's so *petty*!' Vivienne exploded.

What she was waving in one hand, Alix saw, was a piece of paper. It had the look of a club flyer. She cocked an eyebrow, one hand resting on her hip. After a moment, Vivienne's lips flattened into a thin line and she handed the small piece of paper over.

Not a club flyer, Alix saw. A telephone booth advert. Done in shaky black and white photocopying, it showed a smudged photo of a woman with her arms over her head, tied to a wooden frame. Her legs were also lashed to the frame, spread wide apart. She was suspended over a giant dildo, the head of it inches from her arse.

'What the hell?' Alix said. Fern appeared at her shoulder, resting a warm arm around Alix's waist, and reading aloud from the print:

' "I am a fancy bitch who will squeal as you punish me. Cum in my face, and ram me up the arse. Hear me scream. No call-back, no waiting. Phone" – that's a college number,' Fern interrupted herself.

'It's my number!' Vivienne said.

'Wow, hot . . .'

Alix elbowed Fern sharply in the ribs. The girl

smelled of leather and female sweat, and she grinned as cute as a sex-pixie, but Alix could happily have slapped her right now. 'It's not "hot" if it's done by someone else who's got it in for you!'

'I am not giving free phone sex that degrades women!' Vivienne Mayhew snapped at the younger girl. 'I've had eight calls this morning. These ads are in phone boxes up and down the High Street, and God knows how far away, too. And you know what? If I complain, I'll just get told I'm investigating sex anyway, so how can I find it distressing!'

The Professor was wearing half of one of her smarter work suits. Alix let her gaze slide up from the ivory leather sandals to the just-above-the-knee ivory linen skirt that snugged around her generous, shapely hips, and the pale gold silk blouse against which her breasts strained with her rapid breathing. Evidently Vivienne Mayhew had been exasperated enough to leave her office without her jacket.

'Sandro Elliot just brought me this.' Vivienne took the paper back from Alix. 'That at least explains what's going on. Obviously I keep an unlisted number, because after *Hidden Pleasure* I did get crank calls. Now that stupid bastard has plastered it over half of London. He knows he can't sabotage this project with the college – it's just spite!'

At the thought of the lanky, tall, blond Sandro also looking at the photo, Alix blushed. She felt herself growing warm. The muscles of her thighs loosened.

'What can we do about it?' she blurted.

The three of them looked at each other. It was Fern who jerked a thumb towards her bike, and began shrugging back into her leathers. 'We can start taking them out of local call boxes to begin with . . .'

Alix nodded. She saw Vivienne nod her own agreement, but the older woman's gaze was distant.

'Now it's personal,' Vivienne said. 'I won't risk any more difficulty with this project. Jordan has got to be *stopped*.'

Alix picked the last of the stickers carefully off the inside of the phone box's transparent plastic walls.

'You don't need to bother doing all that!' Fern Barrie appeared, from further down the road. She brandished a fistful of paper strips. 'Just tear out the bit with the phone number on. *Why* is he being such an arsehole?'

'Now why didn't I think of that?' Alix stared at the girl's hand. She began to pick curls of sticky paper out from under her short fingernails. 'I don't blame Vivienne for being pissed off about this – I'd be livid if it was *my* number! And there's no way we can be sure we've got all of them . . .'

'She can change her number.'

'With all the business problems *that* involves.'

'Oh. Yeah.'

The sun coming out from behind a cloud sprawled fresh light over the South London streets. A rush of cars and a number of pedestrians went by, not noticing two students hanging around a public phone in Lewisham.

'And I don't know what's biting Jordan Axley,' Alix added. 'For all I know, he's a professional arsehole. Maybe he's just jealous of Vivienne because she's been on TV.'

'Shame we couldn't all have talked to Fran and Jael before they went back up north.'

'You think we'd have spent much time talking?'

Fern's pixie face split into a wicked grin. 'Guess not. That Jael, she sounds *way* cool. And Professor Axley's sister. How come you get to be there when that happens!'

Alix slid an arm around Fern's waist, grinning. The younger woman's flesh was firm and warm under her touch. Alix said, 'Just lucky, I guess . . .'

A passing car honked its horn. Fern, without looking in that direction, held out one hand with the middle finger extended.

'We have to do something about him,' Fern added.

'Blackmail?'

'Hey, *yeah*!'

'I was joking,' Alix said hastily. She began to walk back to the bike with Fern beside her. 'What does he do that we could blackmail him for? And *don't* say "inappropriate relations with a student". Fixing that on him would be seriously naff.'

Fern unslung the helmet from her bike, and handed Alix the spare from the pannier. She lifted her leg over and sat down – seemingly tiny on the 1000 cc machine, but (as Alix had cause to know) entirely in control of it.

'He doesn't have relations!' Fern protested. 'Word is, he doesn't try it on with the girls or the boys. And he doesn't date anyone else on the staff. And nobody's heard any rumours. I reckon he doesn't do it at all!'

'You're joking?' Alix heard her own voice becoming muffled as she put the helmet on. To herself, she muttered, 'No wonder he doesn't like what Vivienne's doing.'

As she sat down astride the big bike, leather saddle pushing up into her crotch, an idea hit her. She ignored Fern reaching back to tug at her wrist, wanting her to put her arms around Fern's waist.

No wonder he doesn't like what Vivienne's doing . . .

She reached up and ripped her helmet off. Fern leaned around, trying to look at her. She pounded on

Fern's back with her free hand, then pointed at the helmet. After a second, Fern took hers off.

'What?' The bright sunlight was making Fern blink. Her hair stood up in a collection of hedgehog spikes. Frustrated, she all but bounced on the bike saddle. '*What?*'

'How does he look at you?'

'Huh?' Fern looked bewildered.

'In lectures, tutorials, how does he look at you?'

'He doesn't.' The younger girl's body relaxed. She swivelled on the bike's saddle, looking curiously at Alix. 'You know . . . he really doesn't. I don't think he's asked me a question in tutorials for weeks. And at the start of the year, I couldn't say enough for him. Hey, maybe what I'm doing with Professor Mayhew makes him disgusted?'

'Maybe, but I've got a better idea.' Alix reached out and slid her hand into the breast of Fern's leathers. Her fingers touched hot, smooth skin and the skimpiest of crop-tops.

'That *is* a better idea, but is it going to solve the problem?'

Regretfully, Alix removed her hand. 'No. But what I'm thinking might. If he can't look at you now . . . he might be disgusted by your behaviour. But he might *not*. He might be feeling something else entirely. And if he is . . . then blackmail is a real possibility.'

What Vivienne Mayhew drove, surprisingly enough, was not a new car. It was a battered, fifteen-year-old Volvo estate, the sun showing up all the minor dents in the bodywork. Still, there were few enough people around it in the car park that Alix could be easy about not being overheard.

'I thought we'd better talk to you,' she said. The

sun, blasting down, made the flesh of her shoulders hot to the touch. For a second she wished for somewhere cool to escape to. 'You know him better than either of us. You've worked with him. Do you think I'm right?'

Vivienne Mayhew reached up and took off her sunglasses. She squinted at Alix. In the white light, you could see the lines at her eyes. It made her seem not old, but easy in her flesh.

'That Jordan is jealous of more than my being "famous"?' The older woman put the term in audible quotes. 'That's . . . an interesting thought. I've assumed he resents the fact that Philosophy is unlikely to get his face on television. If it isn't *that* that he resents—'

'Alix thinks he's just jealous,' Fern interrupted. 'We're getting laid and he's not!'

Other students' sandals and trainers crunched on the gravel of the car park. A couple of boys (or at least Alix thought of them so) passed close enough to wave, and simultaneously check out Fern Barrie. The younger woman looked past and through them. Disappointed, they drifted off.

'That could be,' Vivienne Mayhew admitted. 'He's never mentioned a girlfriend. Or a boyfriend, come to that.'

'He ever hit on you?'

'Fern!' Alix yelped, agonised by embarrassment on the older woman's behalf. She dumped her bag down by her feet to cover her confusion. When she straightened up again, the dark-haired woman was smiling at her and standing a little hipshot, one fist on the hip of her close-fitting ivory linen skirt.

'Do you know, I don't think he ever has.'

'What about Mr Elliot – did he ever ask *him* out?'

'Fern!'

'Oh, stop getting your panties in a push.' Fern grinned at Alix, wiping sweat off her red face. The leathers must be hot in this midday sun, Alix thought. As she did, the girl slid her zip down and skinned out of the jacket. The crimson silk lining rustled. She smelled faintly and wonderfully of sweat: an almost-perfumed odour peculiar to her. Patches of sweat soaked her white top dark.

'So he's not getting any,' Fern said. 'And that's where Alix's idea comes in. If he's not getting any—'

'—he has to be bitterly jealous of you and us because we are,' Alix cut in, determined not to let Fern have the final word. 'And so, naturally, he thinks women going out and doing what they fantasise about is disgusting. Because he's not doing what he fantasises about – if he does fantasise at all.'

The distant college clock struck one. A flight of seagulls, moving out from the river, whirled overhead in a storm of whiteness before skimming off towards Blackheath. Alix, looking northwards, realised for the first time that one of the skyscrapers that stood grey against the hazed horizon was probably the headquarters of CompuForce.

And if anybody in the office knew what I've been doing down here . . . Would they be jealous or would they be terrified?

'So.' Vivienne's voice interrupted her reverie. 'We think he might be jealous of us. What does that mean? Where does it leave us? Because if he is, he won't stop this spiteful sabotage.'

Alix saw Fern bouncing on the toes of her engineer boots, and got her reply in just as the girl opened her mouth.

'We thought we'd blackmail him into stopping,' Alix

said coolly. 'We wondered whether we could borrow your car?'

'There's a fear that is sexual,' Vivienne Mayhew said, her voice low and quiet. 'And there's plain, ordinary terror. If I see that in him . . . then I'm going to call a halt to this. And you'll stop. This isn't a dungeon, and he's not a volunteer: if I say the whole thing's off, it's off. Is that clear?'

Huddled beside Alix in the back of the Volvo, Fern Barrie grumbled, 'Hey, but then how are we going to blackmail him into getting off your back?'

The street lamps were hardly visible against the late sunset sky. Nonetheless, they gave an orange tint to Vivienne Mayhew's skin, where she sat in the driver's seat. Alix spoke before the older woman could.

'This isn't a fantasy.'

'That's right.' In the car's central mirror, Vivienne's eyes met Alix's. 'It isn't. If there's a mess, we have to clear it up. If someone starts to not be able to handle it – we *stop*. Or we don't start this at all. Do you understand?'

'Aw, yeah, okay.' Fern subsided into the back seat. She slouched down. The collar of her leather jacket pushed her soft spikes of hair up at the back of her neck. The shadows hid her expression. Her voice said, 'I don't want to really scare him.' And then a giggle. 'Unless that's what he likes.'

'There are certain signs that make that obvious . . .'

Alix leaned forward in the car seat, and interrupted Professor Mayhew. 'There he is. That's him.'

Jordan Axley's daily commute took him by train almost to the north side of the M25. The Volvo rested unobtrusively down one of the many side streets of two-storey terraced houses, its colour not showing clearly in the sunset light. From where it was parked, Alix could see the station exit.

And that's him all right. Going back to his house. His cat – does he have a cat? No: too sensual. Back to his house and his books . . .

'If this doesn't work, we're going to look *so* stupid,' Alix muttered.

Fern grinned. 'What can go wrong?'

'Never say that!'

For a moment, Alix's stomach was convulsed with terror. An ordinary street just off the main road – a bank, and a small supermarket further down – the essence of normality. If things happen, usually, it's things going wrong. Two cars tailgating. A scrap after the pub turns out that gets heated and someone gets hurt.

'Let's not fuck this up,' she murmured under her breath.

'It's easier in fantasy, isn't it?' Without waiting for a reply, Vivienne turned the key in the ignition. She pulled a black knee-length stocking down over her face and when she turned to squint at Alix, her features were distorted, unrecognisable. 'Go on!'

Alix did the same thing, hurriedly pulling the stocking over her head. It split and laddered. She swore, ripped it off and stepped out of the car, into the quiet road, and squatted down behind the rear of the vehicle.

On the far side of the car, she heard the other door close. Leaning down and squinting, she saw high heels tapping the pavement – Fern had got out of the car.

Heart in her dry mouth, Alix began to creep towards the back of the car. Footsteps sounded in the street from the direction of the station. Fern's voice said, 'Hey, mister. Want some company?'

The street light helped her, Alix suddenly realised. She could see Fern's shadow cast across the road – and a second shadow: Jordan Axley's, further off. When Fern spoke, the second shadow slowed . . . stopped.

'What *do* you think you're doing?' His voice sounded exasperated. 'Fern – Miss Barrie? I hope this isn't one of your ridiculous adventures!'

Oh bugger, he's recognised her!

Alix stood up, moving forward in the car's shadow. He should not have recognised Fern. She could see the girl's long blonde wig from here, and she knew that the pancake makeup ought to have made her look like a sex-worker – but not like herself.

'So what if it is?' Fern's voice came after a pause. 'So what if I fantasise about being a prossie? You could be my trick.'

It seemed to stop him in his tracks. As Alix came around the end of the car, she could see why. The girl was wearing high black stilettos and a pale tan mac that hung open from her shoulders. In the opening, light gleamed on a lot of skin. Her pelmet-skirt didn't cover the tops of her stockings, and her tight, crimson sequinned top just enclosed her boobs.

Alix realised that Jordan Axley was staring, not looking at anything else but Fern. Now she was standing almost next to his six-foot-one or -two height, any idea of bundling him into the car seemed ridiculous. And it would be only seconds before he noticed her—

Fern reached out a hand on which the nails were enamelled bruise-purple. She took the tie out of Jordan Axley's jacket and held on to the end. 'Don't tell me you've never been with a working girl . . .'

Oh Gawd, what do I do!

We ought to back out, here, because he's seen Fern

now. If nothing else happens, she can pass it off as an attempt to make a fantasy come true . . .

Just as she put one foot back to start to sneak away, she saw a darkness come down over Jordan Axley's head. In a split second, she realised that it was a hessian sack, that Vivienne Mayhew had done it and was now dragging it down over his shoulders; that Fern Barrie had stepped forward and thrown her arms around him, pinning his arms to his side—

She had a moment in which she saw herself run. A quick sprint to the station, a ticket into town; back to the flat and forget all about this. *Nothing to do with me; I wasn't there.*

And maybe I would have done, a few weeks ago.

The key awkward in her hand, she unlocked the back door of the Volvo, thrust it upwards, and stood back as the other two women forced Axley to bend over, half in and half out of the car. His cries were muffled, but could still be heard. Alix stepped around them, grabbed his ankles, and lifted. She felt his body quiver under her hands as they rolled him.

'Go!' she whispered.

Crawling in behind Fern, bumping knee and elbow, she hauled the door down behind her, and staggered and fell on top of Jordan Axley as the car shot off out into the main road.

Chapter Twelve

MUFFLED SHOUTS STILL ECHOED from the direction of the garage.

Not that anyone is going to hear him, Alix thought, with relief.

This house, set far out in the Home Counties countryside, had no other buildings within a couple of miles – unless you counted the couple of falling-down old barns.

'Good thing Alan let you use this place,' she said.

Vivienne's lips moved in a smile. 'After the last time I saw them ... it really *did* get rid of the hostility, you know? Alan didn't even ask why I needed the house.'

'I wonder if Axley's out of the car yet,' Alix mused.

'Doubt it. Those things are tanks.' Fern Barrie stripped her mac off. She followed that by stripping her sequinned boob tube off over her head, and stepping out of her shortie-skirt. She dropped both garments on the back of one of the living room's comfortable sofas. Dressed only in stockings and suspenders, she bent over to rummage in the sports bag she had brought in with her from the car.

That is *some* ass! Alix thought. If not for the presence of Vivienne Mayhew – and the shouting man in the garage – she would have reached over and slid her hand across the cute, slim ass-cheeks in front of her, and pushed her fingers down into the warm wetness of the girl's cleft.

'What the hell do we do now though?' Alix asked. 'He's recognised Fern. Even if we're disguised—' she pointed at the black latex garments spread over the other couch '—he can probably make a good guess at who the rest of us are.'

Vivienne Mayhew was standing beside the couch. She squinted out of the diamond-paned window at the last of the sunset light and the blue shadows of evening. Turning back, she reached down and picked up a full head mask, letting it slither through her fingers.

'I don't know about you, Alix,' she confessed, 'but I would feel remarkably silly wearing this in front of someone who knows me! We thought he would be disorientated, dazed . . .'

'He's still ours.' Fern finished hauling on a pair of black jeans. The *wck!* of the zip was loud in the quiet. She was now wearing a black T-shirt with quarter-sleeves, Alix saw. Barefoot, and with her scruffy hair spiked up in a brown halo, she looked more like anybody's kid sister than the hooker of ten minutes before.

' "Ours"?' Vivienne Mayhew queried.

'He still doesn't know where he is. He still doesn't have a wallet. He can't leave here unless one of us unlocks the garage door. He's still ours.'

Alix began to smile, slowly. 'You know, she's right.'

'But I don't see – afterwards—'

'Don't worry about the disguises,' Alix suggested, and went on, ignoring the Professor's interruption. '*Let* him see who we are. If we're right, it'll work better that way. He knows you could gossip to all the college staff and Fern could spread the word around the students. He's going to have every reason to keep his mouth shut.'

Vivienne Mayhew said, '*If* we're right.'

'Oh, sure: if. If he's a fundie with a real hatred for sex . . .' Alix shrugged. 'Then he's already seen Fern, and . . .'

Vivienne completed: 'And it isn't too big a jump from that to guess at you or me. Which is why I think we should call a halt to this now and let him go.'

Fern kicked at the lush carpet with her bare heel. Having her breasts and shoulders concealed by the soft black brushed cotton of the T-shirt was, if anything, *more* sexy, Alix realised. Fern muttered, 'And we're not even going to see if he responds?'

'We could be up on a charge of assault.'

At that thought, the three of them were quiet for a moment. The gas-jet fire hissed in the artificial inglenook. Alix felt the fine fair hairs on her arms start to prickle up. From the garage, a renewed burst of shouting echoed.

'Yeah, well, we might just be up on an assault charge anyway . . .' Fern's voice trailed off sulkily.

What is it today: Tuesday? There's EastEnders *on TV. A takeaway supper back at the flat.* That's *real life – not sitting out here in some townie's idea of a country farmhouse, with a respected professor of philosophy locked in the garage! This whole thing is crazy!*

Alix found herself beginning to smile again. *But I am crazy . . .*

'What is it, Alix?' Vivienne Mayhew asked.

'I'm with Fern,' Alix said slowly. 'He's ours.'

'But—'

'No, listen,' Alix interrupted. She felt the same tingle in the pit of her belly that she had felt stepping into the Marquis of Granby, or moving forward to kiss Fran Axley on her warm, red lips. 'You've chosen us because we're women who are willing to put our fantasies into practice. Well, I'm still willing. I have a number of things I'd like to do to Jordan Axley. And I'll risk the assault charge, because I think I'm right – he's jealous of what we're doing, and he's never going to admit that *that*'s why this happened to him.'

The gas fire hissed loudly. Its warmth permeated the chill air. She found herself huddling into the spare leather biker-jacket that Fern had lent her. She perched herself on the edge of the sofa, pushing the latex body-coverings off on to the rug.

'Never mind Jordan Axley,' she said. 'When are we going to get another chance to do something like this?'

Fern looked up from under dark lashes, her clear eyes holding more practical intelligence than her usual fluffhead manner. 'And it's worth it if there's a fuss and you get kicked out of your job?'

'Who cares? I'm not going back there anyway.'

Alix stopped.

She stood up again, hugging the heavy leather jacket around herself. With one hand she reached up and tugged at the pins that held her hair, letting it spill down on to her shoulders in a silver mass. Slowly, almost in awe of the words, she repeated, 'I'm not going back there anyway . . .'

'*Wow!*'

'I'll finish the course, because there's stuff on it I can use. And I'll cover the tuition fees. But I'm going back to being a consultant,' Alix said, grinning now. 'They can take their nine-to-five and stick it where the sun doesn't shine!'

'Woo-hoo!' Fern gave a shrill whistle that bounced off the imitation Jacobean beams. 'Way to go, that woman!'

Vivienne Mayhew, looking a little concerned, said, 'Alix, are you sure?'

'I'm sure! In a few months I can get back to the cutting edge of the field. I'm done with that sort of "security".' Alix stretched her shoulders, feeling it almost as a physical weight dropping away. 'I'm not scared of going freelance again. Not now. I've done so much in the last few weeks, it would be ridiculous to sit around in an office being scared of risk!'

Slowly, Vivienne Mayhew's face creased into a smile. The lines that worry had put there mostly faded. Wearing the light summer coat that she had donned over her suit for the drive, she looked almost respectable – until you saw that face, Alix thought. The older woman put her fists on her hips. Her dark brunette hair, done up in a thick braid, swung down her back. Her smile made her eyes flash black and brilliant.

'Well, so it would,' she said softly.

'Oh, *yes*!' Fern bounced on her bare feet and then bent to scrabble for her combat boots. 'Alix, what's the plan?'

'Bring some of the equipment in your bag,' Alix directed. 'Professor, if he hasn't got out of the car yet, back it up into one of those old barns.'

The light of hurricane lanterns brought a circle of light to the centre of the dark barn. It was just enough to see the rusting machinery, bales of straw, and the beams that had once separated stock pens from each other and now stood bare, cemented into the concrete floor.

Alix unlocked the tailgate of the Volvo estate and hurriedly stepped back.

The tall, lean figure of Jordan Axley shot out of the car. He almost tripped, getting what must have been cramped legs to take his weight. He stared around. Alix met his gaze. He looked at her as if this was something crazy: the world of things that only happen in Sunday tabloids.

'Miss Neville.' His voice sounded creaky. He coughed. 'Miss Neville . . .'

'Don't talk,' she said. 'Not yet.'

'*What*—!'

Alix stepped forward out of the dimness at the limit of the lanterns' light. She saw his eyes widen a little. There was nothing unusual about what she wore – it was still Fern's spare biker jacket and a fairly conservative calf-length black wraparound skirt. It must be what she held in her hand. A fleece-lined metal cuff . . . with about twelve inches of chain and another cuff hanging free from the other end.

'Put your wrists out.'

'Oh really!'

'Put—' she let her voice drop back to normal '—your wrists out.'

He still impressed her with his height and his weight. He might have been a little on the lean side, but he was still strong with it, and a good head taller than her. And a handful of years older. She kept her eyes on his. Shaking one hand, she made the heavy chain-links rattle.

'Give me your hands.'

'What *is* this?'

Alix took a deep breath and said, 'You know what it is.'

A flicker of some expression passed across his sharp features. It was enough. She let herself smile again: a friendly, knowing look.

'What?' she said. 'You think Fern's the only one? We all have our fantasies, Professor.'

She saw his gaze waver. He was looking around, checking the barn, not seeing the doors – they were outside the sphere of golden light – but a little reassured, all the same, by something as mundane as the presence of a car.

'Is that who's with you? Miss Barrie and another one of her student friends?'

'You could say that.'

She saw his Adam's apple bob. He said, 'Well, nice as that compliment is, I'd be obliged if you'd call me a taxi. If you do, we'll say no more about it.'

'Give me your hand,' Alix repeated. The cold air of the barn smelled of chaff and concrete, but she felt herself sweating inside the biker jacket. A warmth was growing between her legs. She smiled. 'Give me one wrist. Just . . . see what it feels like, that's all.'

'Oh, really, this is ridiculous!'

'What have you got to lose?'

His gaze went past her again. She saw the velvet black pupils of his eyes dilate. He was looking for Fern, she realised, and Fern's hypothetical 'friend'. He made some show of brushing himself down, straightening his suit jacket, and then fixed her with a sharp glare. 'My coat? My wallet?'

'Indoors.' Using her thumb, Alix flicked open the metal cuff. It was heavy and a good quarter-inch thick. The sheepskin lining that cushioned the hard metal would be welcome, she thought, after not very long. She reached out her other hand for his arm.

'Feel what it's like, that's all . . .'

This was it, the moment – reality on one side, fantasy on the other – and she recognised it. He would walk away and hammer on the doors of the barn or he would let her take his arm, consenting through inaction.

Her hand closed over his sleeve. She felt an instant's tightening of the muscle, and then she felt it come towards her. Jordan Axley stood with his right arm stretched out, a semi-contemptuous smile on his lips, *If you must play these childish games* plain on his face.

She snapped the cuff together over his wrist.

For a second they both looked at it. Solid metal, closed around shirt-cuff and the bottom of his jacket sleeve. Too tight to slide out of. He flexed his hand, turning it like a man trying on a new watch, looking at it from several angles. The heavy chain swung, the other cuff jingling on the end of it.

'Do you remember a conversation . . .' Alix kept her voice low and level. 'About how people fantasise . . . and some people fantasise about being tied up and masturbated to a climax . . .'

His voice sounded dry. 'I remember.'

'But the question is, who wants to be tied and who wants to do the tying . . .' She reached down and caught the swinging metal cuff and clicked it open.

There was a perceptible pause. The day's heat had left a little warmth in the air. Almost, you could smell the ancient odours of animals from when this had been a working barn. The lamps' sphere of light provided an illusion of privacy, all else outside it hidden in the dark. Jordan Axley, in his dark suit, seemed at once very real and very out of place. She continued to watch him.

Very slowly, as if he couldn't quite believe what he was doing, he held out his other arm, offering his wrist.

She smiled.

Moving with absolute confidence, she reached up, pulling his cuffed arm over his head, and flicked the chain and cuff over a beam overhead. Some dust trickled down. She had to stand on her toes to catch the manacle again, and then she reached down and pulled his free hand up and fumbled for long agitated seconds before she got the catch to click home.

He stood with his arms drawn up over his head, the stress pulling the line of his jacket askew. She reached out and undid his buttons, one by one ... until the suit jacket swung open, displaying his lean, strong body in a sweat-stained pale blue shirt, and with the smallest of bulges in the crotch of his trousers.

He said nothing, but his eyes did not move from her face.

She stepped back.

Slowly, out of the darkness, she was aware of the others moving forward. First Fern, still in black jeans and T-shirt, but with a stout pair of boots on, and a short many-thonged whip hanging off her wrist on a lanyard. She saw Axley's eyes open wide at that. A rush of colour went up his face, and he shifted his head and neck as if his collar and tie were suddenly too tight. She saw him shift his body around a little, as if he could hide the growing bulge at his crotch.

Out of the shadow, a dark-haired woman stepped into the light. She might have been any townie living in the country, with a light-coloured conservative jacket on against the chill, but it was her face that took Jordan Axley's attention.

'*Vivienne!*'

He twisted his body away, until he was looking over his shoulder at the woman. Alix moved forward. He tried to turn again, realised he couldn't hide himself from all of them, and stood still, sweating. Now a gigantic hard-on poked at the front of his trousers, straining at the material.

'No!' he said at last. 'I won't let you do this! What is

it – photographs? I'll have you up on assault charges! Nobody will believe anything you say!'

Vivienne Mayhew's voice was low and thrilling. 'Oh, what do you think we are, Jordan? There won't be any assault. There won't be any photographs.'

'Then . . .' He slipped, slightly, as one of his shoes slid on the concrete. The chain took his full weight until he got his balance. The cuffs pulled over his sleeves and settled around his wrists. He yanked twice, hard, at the beam he was chained to. Nothing happened but a sifting-down of dust that made him cough. 'What – what's – all this for?'

The older brunette ignored him. She seated herself carefully on one of the bales of hay, as if she were an audience. Fern Barrie came further forward into the light.

'We just want to show you something,' she said. 'We want to show you what you're missing. Alix . . . get your kit off.'

Jordan Axley blinked. He would be beginning to get cramps in his shoulder joints about now, Alix thought. She watched him, as she reached up to slide off her borrowed leather jacket.

Underneath it, a tight leather bodice was laced over her small round breasts, flattening them cruelly against her body. The flesh, forced up, formed a deep, high cleavage. She undid the ties on the long skirt that she wore, and dropped it to the floor. Under that, she wore Fern's short black leather skirt, which hardly covered her to the bottom of her buttocks. She knew her red silk knickers must be plainly visible.

'Put your hands up.'

Fern's voice came from behind her. Still with her eyes on Jordan Axley, Alix lifted her arms obediently, and felt the snick of cuffs closing snugly around her wrists. A sharp yank dragged her up on her toes and she felt herself swing, suspended from the same beam.

'Some people just get lucky,' Fern's voice said. 'You get to watch, Professor Axley.'

Alix dangled, only barely able to get a grip on the concrete flooring with her toes. The bodice held her so tightly now that it was a strain to breathe. And not being able to bring her arms down made her feel absolutely helpless. The short skirt rode up her buttocks, showing even more of her knickers, and she squirmed a little, trying to persuade the skirt back down.

Out of nowhere, a sudden *thwack!* caught her across both buttocks.

'Oh shit!' The gasp was knocked out of her.

The white-hot sting of the whip thongs wasn't pain, wasn't pleasure; it was pure sexual heat. She felt herself instantly wet. The crotch of her knickers became sopping. Juices spread between her thighs.

She could see nothing of what went on behind her. She kept her eyes on Jordan Axley. His mouth had fallen open. Great patches of sweat marked the underarms of his shirt where his jacket was pulled up to expose them. His cock was throbbing in his pants, and she could see a small dark stain of pre-come on the fabric.

Thwack!

The thongs bit home into the flesh of her buttocks. She winced, twisting as she hung. The heat of it spread across her skin, and deep into the muscle beneath. She heard herself groan. The ache of unsatisfied lust made her groin throb.

'You can't do that!' Jordan Axley's voice said.

Not aware until then that she had shut her eyes, Alix opened them. The snug, fleece-lined cuffs gripped her arms just below the wrist-bone. She felt held, contained. And looking at Axley's expression, now that he began to jerk his arms down – achieving only the slide of the chain along the beam – he felt the same way. Restrained only to be released.

'I *can* do it,' Fern Barrie said. She walked around to a point where Alix could see her. The black T-shirt and black jeans were more of a turn-on than any dominatrix outfit could have been. Being everyday clothes, they enhanced the reality of what was going on.

'And,' Fern added, her gaze still on Jordan Axley, 'she can't do anything about it . . .'

A flick of her wrist, and the eighteen-inch leather thongs slashed across the top of Alix's breasts. Alix gasped a breath of air, sucking vainly for a second. Lines of white heat scored her tits, and the leather corset held her bound and tight. She swayed and sagged in her chains, dimly aware of the throbbing heat between her thighs: the pain of wanting.

'Whatever I do, she has to take it . . .'

Alix blinked tears from her eyes. She watched Fern reverse the whip in her hand. The handle was slick black wood, carved in the form of a cock. Slowly, the younger woman approached. She reached out and teased the hem of Alix's skirt up with the tip of the dildo-handle. Then, carefully, she put it down the front of Alix's panties, and used it to pull them down to her knees.

Hot, wet and sweating, Alix hung from the wrist-cuffs. She couldn't help her hips swaying towards the carved whip-handle.

'. . . And nothing happens until I say it does,' Fern finished. 'What about it, Professor? Do I shove this up her cunt?'

Jordan Axley's body twitched in its chains. Alix saw

his face flush a dark, deep red. He hung his head, the sound of his breathing now echoing through the barn. A large, wet dark stain spread across the front of his trousers.

'Just the thought of it,' Fern marvelled. 'Just the words. Woo-hoo! Way to go, Professor Axley!'

'Never mind *him*—' Alix could only gasp. 'I want it now. Do me, you little bitch!'

'Ask nicely.'

'Do me, you bitch, or when I get out of this, I'll fuck you until your face turns blue!'

'Oh, we're not co-operative, are we? We're not polite . . .' Fern Barrie turned on her heel, looking speculatively up at Jordan Axley's wrist-cuffs. Alix knew vaguely in the back of her mind that the girl might be thinking of freeing the man. It meant nothing to her. Only the searing emptiness between her legs meant anything. Only the throb of her clit, able to come now from the merest brush or touch . . .

'Please!' Alix begged.

Fern turned away from the hanging man. She gave Alix a straight look from under her short, urchin-cut hair. Alix feasted her eyes on the curve of the girl's back, the neat sleekness of her hips.

In two steps, Fern was standing next to her. She put her hand behind Alix's head, burying it in the masses of silver-blonde hair. Alix felt her head pulled forward. Fern's lips met hers, Fern thrusting her tongue into Alix's mouth, twining her tongue, probing, thrusting until she was halfway down Alix's throat, it seemed.

Dizzy, Alix felt the whip handle parting her thighs. She could barely get a grip on the ground with her feet. She dangled. The cool, hard wood slid up her slick thighs and probed inward. She felt it at the lips of her cunt. It slid back and forth, teasing the outside of her lips; then rolled and slid over the clitoris hood, one hard stroke—

'God!' Alix screamed. The orgasm thundered through her. She felt her knees go weak, and she hung suspended only by her wrists, as the heat and flush of pleasure scalded out from her groin to her fingertips. 'Oh *God*!'

Somebody spoke; somebody else answered: she could not tell anything about it. As she panted and her breathing slowed, she found her body shaking and chilled.

Hands at the cuffs unlocked them. Her arms fell to her sides, numb; then she swore as circulation flooded back in. She was dimly aware of a coat around her shoulders, of being helped a few steps.

'Sit down. No, here. On the bale.'

Alix looked up. Vivienne Mayhew sat down beside her, putting a warm arm around her shoulders. Alix stared into the lush features, the gold-dark eyes, for a long moment. She grinned, shakily. 'That was something...'

'It certainly was.'

Alix turned her head. Jordan Axley hung from the chains, his arms up but his feet resting securely on the concrete. His head hung down, dark hair flopping over his forehead. Fern Barrie was standing in front of him. She held the whip handle in one hand, sticky with Alix's own juices, and trailed the thongs of the whip through her other hand.

'Just seeing it makes you come in your pants,' she was saying.

'It's – disgusting! Cruel – abusive—'

'She *asked* me for it.'

'I don't care!' Jordan Axley lifted his sweating face. His eyes avoided Fern. Accidentally, his gaze caught

Alix's. She smiled at him, as she leaned back against Vivienne's shoulder for support, her whole body tingling with the aftermath of release.

He looked away from her, hurriedly.

'And you stand there with your underpants full of cum and tell me you don't like it?' Fern sounded astounded.

If it was possible, Alix saw, Jordan Axley was blushing a deeper red. He wiped his wet forehead against his arms, and moisture marked the arms of the suit jacket. She glanced down. Some pressure from inside was pushing out his fly.

Already? Wow. I didn't think he had it in him . . .

Alix snuffled back a giggle. Vivienne's arm tightened around her. The warmth and perfumed odour came clearly to her over the smells of the barn and the scent of sex in the air.

'Are you all right?' Vivienne asked.

'Yes . . . I was just looking at Jordan. He's ready again!'

'So he is . . .'

Fern Barrie's clear voice came through the lantern light and cool air. 'All you have to do is what Alix did – ask for what you want.'

'No!' He shook his head, wet hair flying. 'I don't want that! I don't!'

Alix saw the younger girl begin to pace around him, her boots clicking on the concrete. Jordan Axley twisted his head, trying to see her over his shoulder. He lost his footing for a second and slipped, his fall arrested by the chain over the beam. An expression of pain and shame passed across his face.

'Let me go,' he whispered, regaining his footing. 'I won't tell anyone what you've done.'

Fern trailed the thongs through her hand. As she

walked around in front of him again, prowling like a big cat, she slapped the thongs down into her palm. Her lips skinned back from her teeth in an expression of both pain and pleasure.

'Who cares what you say? Who'll believe you?'

Alix turned her head, grinned at Vivienne Mayhew, and slipped the coat off her shoulders. She stood up and paced towards the chained man. Stiletto heels clinked on the concrete as she walked. He shot a hurried look at her, and then hung his head again, cheeks blazing.

'What do you want?' Alix said quietly. 'Do you want to tie me up, and make me come? Or do you want to be tied up and have us make you come?'

The cloth of his fly leapt at her words. She saw his cock outlined clearly under the material. Thick, heavy and long... She smiled. She reached one hand towards his zip, then let her arm fall back to her side. 'Like Fern says, *nothing happens unless you ask for what you want...*'

'What?' He glared at them, dazed, face running with sweat. 'No. You have to let me go sooner or later. I'm not telling you anything. This is vile!'

Alix shrugged, aware of how it made her breasts move in the tight leather bodice she was laced into. 'So you don't like being tied up?'

'No!'

'And you don't like watching someone else being tied up and fucked?'

'No!'

'You're a liar.' Alix pointed to the drying stain on his pants. '*That* says you're a liar. Your cock says you're a liar. You don't think it's disgusting at all – you *want* it.'

'I...' His voice cracked. He looked up into the darkness outside the circle of lantern light, as if it were a refuge. Then he dropped his gaze to Alix again. '*You* wanted it. I'm not like you!'

'No?'

A long sigh shuddered through Jordan Axley's whole body. When he looked at her again, his expression was pitiful. The blood drained from his face, taking him from flushed to white in a second. He stood, mutely miserable, his arms pinned above his head, helpless to move.

'All right.' His voice was barely above a whisper. 'All right . . . Do what you have to do. Get it over with.'

Fern's voice cracked out, 'You're not *listening*!' She stood with one foot up on a piece of rusty machinery. She slapped the thongs of the whip against the side of her boot. Jordan Axley quivered.

'You have to ask,' Alix said softly. Something in his face moved her to pity. But that was not the only sensation: she felt a growing warmth again in her crotch, and the image of this man on his knees before her went through her mind. 'If you don't ask – we don't do. What do you want?'

Jordan Axley shut his eyes. There was a silence. Alix stood perfectly still. There was no movement anywhere in the barn, except the shifting cool summer evening air. Jordan slumped, the movement stretching his arms even higher. He opened his eyes again, looking straight at Alix.

'I want . . . I want to be fucked,' he whispered. 'I want you to chain my legs, as well as my hands. I want you to make me helpless. I want you to take my trousers down and fuck me up the arse.'

His voice shook and his face coloured again, but his gaze didn't shift. Alix held her place. She was aware of Fern bending down to her bag, and the clink of metal made her think Fern had found more fetters. She held

Jordan Axley's blue gaze and let herself smile a little.

'Well, well, well . . .' Alix said. 'You want to be chained up and had like a woman.'

His lips pressed together in a pale, hard line. He sniffed. A drop of clear liquid dripped off the end of his nose. There was a suspicious shininess at the corners of his eyes: he might have been weeping. He didn't stop looking at her.

'I want to be made to come.' His voice grated rustily. 'Now you've made me say it . . . you've got to do it. Please!'

Fern knelt to close leg-manacles around his ankle. She trailed the chain around an upright beam, whipping it round twice, and cuffed his other ankle. 'Oh, now, would we just chain you up and walk away? Would we do that?'

'We might do that,' Alix added. She grinned, far more relaxed than she had been a minute ago. 'We might just do . . . nothing. Go back in the house for a cup of coffee. Unlock you in the morning. Maybe we'd even lend you some of Vivienne's husband's clothes, so you don't have to go on a train with your trousers covered in cum.'

'Please, you can't—'

'We can.'

'No!' He tried to move forward, but the ankle-chain restrained him. He could not move his feet more than eighteen inches apart. He yanked both arms down sharply, and Alix saw the edges of the metal cuff press whitely into his flesh, despite the padding.

'Maybe we won't,' Alix said, purringly smooth. 'Maybe . . .'

Tears glistened in the corners of his eyes now. The lean face was suffused with blood. She looked at him hanging, his precise posture lost, his neat dark suit messed up. A smile tugged at one corner of her lips.

'You were jealous,' she said. 'That's all. Jealous of women doing what you only dreamed about. Isn't that right?'

Jordan Axley didn't answer immediately. He tested his ability to move again. As he did so, Fern yanked at the chain on his wrists, pulling it tighter. His feet almost left the ground. He was left helpless, standing on tiptoe.

His gaze went past Alix, out into the lantern light.

He said, 'I want her to do it.'

Alix turned her head. Vivienne Mayhew sat on the straw bale, perfectly still. In her formal ivory linen skirt and jacket, she could have been at any college board meeting. There was no change in her expression as she looked at the panting, sweating shamed man hanging in chains before her.

'Why Vivienne?'

Jordan Axley licked at his lips. 'Because she has something to pay back. Those cards in telephone boxes ... I want to be punished by someone who *means* it.'

Alix caught sight of Fern Barrie's face and saw an expression of outrage.

'*We* can mean it!' the girl protested. She dusted her hands against her jeans and reached for the whip hooked at her belt.

'No, he's right. It's personal.' Alix remembered Vivienne Mayhew's expression in the car park. '*It's personal ...*'

As she spoke, Vivienne got to her feet. She did not remove her jacket. Instead, she walked across the concrete floor with her court shoes tapping on the concrete and only a very small swing to her lush hips. She paused in front of Jordan Axley, looking up into his face.

'Vivienne—'

The older woman grabbed the front of his trousers, clutching a handful of flesh through the fabric, and twisted as she squeezed.

Jordan Axley let out a little high squeak, his eyes bulging.

'Don't you say my name,' Vivienne Mayhew growled, in a rich contralto. 'Don't you *dare.*'

'No, I – no – no, I won't!'

'Never mind what you want. Never mind what you think you want. You're the one who wanted people to phone me and fuck me up the arse . . .'

She let go. Alix watched as the abused flesh swelled in his pants, a hard-on beyond anything he'd had before pushing at the stained fabric. He whimpered aloud.

'Shut up!' Casually, Vivienne bitch-slapped him. 'I didn't tell you you could speak.'

Alix stepped back as Fern came to join her. The golden lantern light gleamed on Vivienne and the chained man. Exchanging glances, they wordlessly agreed on inaction. Alix put her arm around Fern's waist, then slipped her palm up under the soft T-shirt to grab a breast. Fern's hand wandered down between them, hitching up the short, tight leather skirt. Alix felt a finger slide between her lower lips.

'Give me that.' Vivienne held her hand out behind her. Fern put the whip into her palm.

Vivienne Mayhew walked around the helpless man. He strained, trying to watch her. His arms and legs pulled at the chains, but he could only achieve a few inches of movement.

The whip slashed down, catching him across his buttocks. Alix saw the bulge in his pants increase. He sobbed under his breath.

Hands came around his waist from the back. Long olive fingers picked at his waistband, pulling it out a little to get at the top button. The fingers undid the first button, dropped to the zip and tugged it down.

'No . . .' he groaned. 'No, please – please . . .'

His erection jutted out of the open fly of his pants. Vivienne Mayhew walked around to the front of him, grabbed the front of his pants and yanked them down. He squealed, then abruptly stopped, staring at her with wide eyes.

'You're going to take it right up the arse,' Vivienne whispered. 'And any time you think of me in the future, you're going to think of me having you. You're *my* bitch now, Jordan.'

Alix breathed a long, shuddering breath. Fern's nipple hardened under her palm. The finger in her cunt worked her up, getting her hot; but the look on Jordan Axley's face got her hotter. A mixture of shame, pain, and longing – and a desperate desire to come.

Vivienne reversed the whip in her hand, as the girl had done earlier. She stroked the head of the carved cock over Jordan's hairy thighs. His legs shook. Trailing it behind her, she moved around to his back. Alix heard her spit on the whip handle, lubricating it.

She watched Jordan, not Vivienne; watched his eyes widen as he felt the woman's hands on his buttocks, parting his cheeks. A whimper forced itself out between his lips. One leg lifted slightly, pulling tight against the chain. His swollen, thick cock dripped clear liquid.

'Take it, you *girl*!'

Alix saw Vivienne's arm jerk. Jordan Axley's eyes flew wide open. His mouth formed a perfect 'O'. His whole body stiffened. Then, as she began to shove the dildo further up his ass, his eyes closed for a second.

'Fuck me,' he whispered. 'Fuck me up the arse and make me come. I can't stop you. I can't stop you – ahhhh!'

His hips jerked forward. A perfect arc of come jetted into the air, spurting in the light. His body thrashed again, thrusting, his cock pumping out come, his head falling back, his mouth open, giving out a wordless groan.

Thrills shivered through Alix's flesh. Her legs closed together, trapping Fern's finger, and the friction made a succession of tiny orgasms quiver through her, heating her body to warm relaxation.

Vivienne Mayhew walked around in front of Jordan, wiped her hand across his crotch, and then smeared his face with his own cum.

Into the silence, Alix said, 'Aren't you glad there are women learning to put their fantasies into practice?'

Slowly – and a little shakily – Jordan Axley began to smile.

Chapter Thirteen

'TOO LATE!' FERN BARRIE yelped, shooting past Alix in the college lobby. Her arms were piled high with ring-binders. As she spun around to talk to Alix, she kept walking backwards towards the doors. 'Got my first exam on *Friday*!'

'Yes, but I want you—'

'I bet you do!' The girl grinned. Despite the July heat, she was wearing her biker jacket. It hung down over a skirt that wasn't more than a couple of inches longer than it. Her long, smooth bare legs were fully exposed, glistening in the sun. She turned and loped onward.

'—To *talk* to!' Alix finished, as the younger woman shot out through the doors, running to join the group of other first-year students outside: the now-ebullient Adam, and Robbie, and some others Alix didn't know by name.

'Oh, *fine!*' Alix added, aloud, to herself.

She had her own last project to hand in, but that was nine-tenths done. It could be finished off in an evening. No revising necessary.

Just when I could do with a friend to talk to – I suppose I could phone Lewis, but . . .

Thoughts of Lewis Kumar brought the office back

into her mind. She smiled, thinking of exactly how she would frame her resignation. As she turned back, away from the doors and the bright sunlight beyond, she was momentarily dazzled, and banged into somebody.

A muttered curse: a splatter of hot liquid across her hand—

'Shit!' Alix sucked at her hand, between the joint of her thumb and first finger. She looked up at the tall man she had bumped into. He held two cups of cappuccino on a tray. And he was Jordan Axley.

The flavour of the coffee was welcome in her mouth. She couldn't help smiling as she looked up at his dark, severe features. His hooded eyes were expressionless for a moment. Then, shyly, he smiled back at her.

'Sorry.' Her tongue-tip chased a bit of the coffee foam off her full lower lip. 'Ought to look where I'm going. Where are you going with that?'

A slight pink tinge crept across Jordan's face. 'I'm taking them up to Vivienne's office.'

'I see . . .'

There was a glint in his eye, behind the embarrassment. She let her gaze fall for a split second. An outline of his thickening cock was just visible at the crotch of his trousers.

'Need any help?' Alix murmured.

'I wasn't told to bring anyone else. And I believe in doing what I'm told.' His severe mouth softened, momentarily.

Alix thought, *Jordan Axley, you're* flirting!

She grinned at him, this time ruefully. 'Well, have fun! I'm glad somebody's having a good time . . .'

His soft brown eyes took in her expression. 'Wait. I'm sure Vivienne wouldn't mind if you . . . came along to the office. Let me call her and check.'

A lingering warmth pulsed through her groin. The

thought of Jordan Axley tied to Vivienne Mayhew's office chair, helpless to prevent their manipulation of his flesh . . .

'Thanks, but – no, I mean: thanks, really. Maybe next time.'

Jordan lifted a dark eyebrow. He shifted his grip on the tray of cups. 'You're sure?'

'Look . . .' Alix took a deep breath. She smelled the coffee, and the warm London air drifting in through the exit doors. Her entire skin seemed to tingle, wanting – something. The submission of Jordan Axley or the kiss of Vivienne Mayhew; either would be wonderful. *Why am I staying out of this?*

'Do you ever talk to Sandro Elliot?' she asked.

'Our American colleague? Yes.' The tall dark man hesitated for a moment, and then put his tray down on one of the student tables by the door. He seated himself on one of the plastic chairs, and looked at Alix with implicit invitation. She sat down slowly beside him.

'Alessandro Elliot,' Jordan Axley said. 'Yes. What can I tell you? Over here as a teaching assistant; also doing graduate work – on the Victorians, I believe. What is it about him that you want to know?'

Alix took a steadying breath. 'I want to know why he avoids me. I want to know why, when I make a pass at him, he runs a mile! Look, I could tie him up, have him chained up the way you were . . .' Her cheeks flushed at the memory. For a moment, she rubbed her hand down over her T-shirt, feeling the hardening pressure of her nipple under the fine cloth. '. . . And still he wouldn't look at me!'

Looking at Jordan, she could see that his mouth was as dry as hers. His face was warm. He lowered his gaze from hers, almost in shame; but his expression still held a covert joy.

'What's Vivienne going to do to you?' Alix said, diverted, her voice barely loud enough to be heard.

'I'm, ah, not sure. She mentioned something about needing to see me for "academic discipline".'

Tie his hands, bend him over the desk and fuck him up the arse with a dildo!

'Ah, shiiiit . . .' Alix squirmed on the hard plastic seat. Her body heated. The ache of arousal started in her groin. 'Why doesn't Sandro want me to do that to him? Or him to do it to me? Why? I know he fancies me—'

'You do?'

'He got a hard-on the size of the Eiffel Tower! Oh, he wants me,' Alix said. 'But there's something about me he doesn't like – something he won't touch. It's driving me crazy!'

Jordan Axley frowned. 'I don't know.'

'I just wondered if he'd ever, you know, said anything.'

'No . . .' The dark-haired man shook his head. 'In fact, he doesn't talk about you at all. Now I think about it, I find that significant. I . . . don't talk about certain things, you see. Or rather, I didn't.'

Alix spoke without lowering her voice this time. 'But now you're happy to tell everyone you get off on big women making you come?'

'Miss Neville!'

Alix looked at him. 'Isn't that a little – formal?'

Jordan Axley opened his mouth to speak, stopped and let out a small, muffled giggle. He clapped a hand over his mouth. Alix snorted. Laughter tickled inside her, and as she saw Jordan's face, she collapsed against the back of the seat in helpless giggles.

At last Jordan Axley took the precisely folded white handkerchief out of his suit's top pocket, wiped his own eyes carefully and then handed it to her. She copied him. Giggles still bubbled up inside her. She sobered, eventually.

'So he doesn't talk about me,' she said. 'I suppose that's something, but I don't see where it gets me.'

'Nor I.' Jordan stood, bending to pick his tray and frowning. 'It would hardly be the same reason as my own reticence. If I see him, would you like me to broach the subject?'

'Yes. *No!* Oh . . .' Alix shook her head, the loose mass of silver-blonde hair tumbling over her shoulders. 'I don't know! *Damn him!*'

'Quite,' Jordan said dryly. He paused, about to turn away and walk across the lobby. 'As for why he doesn't want to undertake any "academic discipline" – perhaps his tastes don't lie in that direction?'

Alix stood up. She smoothed a strand of her long hair between her fingers. 'I don't know what he likes . . .' She stopped. Speaking slowly, she said again, 'I *don't* know what he likes . . .'

Jordan Axley raised a dark brow.

'No, listen!' Alix said excitedly. 'I don't know, and you don't know, but somebody does – Vivienne does! Because he's been writing down his fantasies for her other group. I wonder if she'd let me read . . .'

Jordan Axley shook his head. 'That would be unprofessional, Miss Neville. No, she wouldn't do that.'

'Ah, shit! I was just thinking . . .' Alix shifted uncomfortably on her high-heeled sandals. 'What if someone *set up* his fantasy for him? Like we did for you . . . He'd have to like it. And if I was the one who set it up for him, maybe *then* he'd like me . . .'

The older man remained with a frown on his face for the moment. Then he looked down at Alix and she thought she saw sympathy in his expression.

'I'm sure we don't have anything to teach you about computer security,' Jordan murmured. 'Suppose I invite Professor Mayhew into *my* office for the next, oh, half an hour, say? Would that be long enough for you to access and read the documents you'd need?'

Alix nodded. 'Thanks,' she said, with a degree of sincerity that made Jordan Axley smile.

'You really want him, don't you?' he said.

'Even if he doesn't want me, I can give him this.' And then Alix smiled, lopsidedly. 'Assuming I'm lucky, and his fantasies don't involve the entire Philharmonic Orchestra and hiring the Albert Hall . . .'

Vivienne Mayhew, arriving back at her office pleasantly relaxed, found an envelope sellotaped to her keyboard. She ripped it open with an ivory-lacquered thumbnail.

> Vivienne, very sorry, have read You Know Who's file – ONLY his!! I know this is well out of order but I HAD to do it. No other way to find out if he'll ever want me. Sorry sorry sorry. Forgive me? Now I don't suppose we'll ever pick up where you and Fran left off.
> Love, A. xxx

After a moment, she began to laugh.

'*Stupid* girl!' she said at last, aloud, and looked around the small cramped office, grinning.

She's smart enough not to have left traces. And I believe her when she says she hasn't read more than Sandro's file. If he complains to me – well, then, I'll tell him to take it up with her.

The relaxation of sexual satisfaction still loosened her muscles, and she stretched her arms out and breathed in deeply, tingling.

'Sort yourself out with your cowboy,' Vivienne murmured, beginning to smile. 'As for the rest . . . well. We'll have to see.'

The sun through the vast plate-glass windows of the Arrivals lounge was blinding. Alix blinked, shaking her head as if she could clear the dazzles out of her vision that way. She felt the sweat soaking into the soft cotton of her sundress, under her arms.

I look lousy, I probably smell and he's not going to turn up anyway, *is* he? Oh fuck!

An endless throng of people pushed past her, with luggage trolleys threatening her ankles. She felt dizzy, trying to take in identifying details of their appearances – so *many* people! – and she stepped back out of the rush for a moment, her eyes fixed on the passport-check desks.

Maybe I should have one of those pieces of paper with a name on to hold up . . .

'Alix?'

The slightly accented deep voice sent a velvet shiver down her spine. In the next second, it was overtaken by panicky butterflies in her stomach: *It's him! It's really him!*

'I, ah,' she cleared her throat and looked at Sandro Elliot where he stood beside her, having just emerged from the crowd. 'I thought you wouldn't come.'

'When somebody sends me an airline ticket through the post . . .'

Sandro was tall: she had to look up to meet his dark blue eyes, gazing down at her. She couldn't read his creased, tanned face at all. He was dressed casually, in jeans and a green cotton shirt with button-down collar, and carried only hand-luggage.

He said, 'You must let me pay you for—'

'No!' she cut in. She heard her voice shaking, and made an attempt to calm herself. 'I had a bunch of money come in unexpectedly – voluntary redundancy money, as it happens.' She grinned. 'I knew there was some reason they sent me off on a training course. And I signed up for the cash *before* I told Human Resources exactly what I'd wanted them to do with their job . . .'

He grinned back. For a second it made him look young and relaxed. As if they were friends, or at any rate people who knew each other, talking about their lives.

Is it because he made his decision without me being there in front of him? Because this is far away from home and it isn't 'real'? If it was this easy, why did he treat me like dirt and avoid me before? – no, don't ask him. Not now. Not yet.

If you sent the ticket back, there was nothing I could do. But I had to ask you.

Biting down hard on all the questions she wanted answers to, Alix merely said with quiet confidence, 'This way . . .'

She turned, walking away on her low-heeled sandals – a good choice, because she felt dizzily unsteady on her feet. *I don't believe it; he's actually here!* She didn't look back to see if he followed. Not until they were outside the terminal in the hot air that smelled of aviation fuel, with the departing jets thundering overhead, did she turn.

Sandro Elliot reached past her to open the door of her taxi.

'Why "Sandro" – "Alessandro", isn't it?' She lowered herself into the car. The grey-blue cotton mini-dress rode up her bare thighs. She felt her skin adhere a little to the leather upholstery.

'Why?' The seat dipped as he sat in beside her. This close, inside the taxi, she could smell his faint odour of male sweat. That and his rumpled fair hair made her want to move in close, fit her body to his . . . she felt the heat of a blush spreading up her face and turned away, staring out of the car window.

'Mexican grandfather,' his voice said. There was mild amusement in it. 'That seems to be all I've inherited from him. Mom's dark. All her kids are blond, like I am.'

The warmth of his thigh beside her – barely an inch away from her own skin – made her flush down her neck. She could feel her nipples hardening a little, inside her dress, just from his closeness, and her bra felt tight. *Oh God, I want him! And we're like strangers!*

She leaned forward, giving the driver instructions, and then made herself lean back as if she felt relaxed.

'Where are we going?' he rumbled.

'You'll find out . . .'

For all the heat outside, and the air-conditioning that now cut in inside the car, all she could smell of herself was the faint musky perfume she had dabbed between her breasts as she was dressing. Nothing overt; nothing to hide – if he was close enough – the scent of woman. She moved a little on the hard leather upholstery, uncomfortable. The warmth in her groin stirred, but didn't flower.

I don't know if he wants me. Surely he wouldn't have come here if . . . Oh, I wish I had the balls to ask him!

The desolate landscape was hemmed in by volcanic rock; nothing to be seen but the road from the airport. Eventually the taxi slowed and began to turn off – Alix saw that the tarmac road came to an end and that they were driving along a mere stony track. Moving down a gear, the vehicle growled on the slope. Ahead, the ridges pulled back to disclose the shimmering sea. Into the silence with only the car's engine roaring, they descended towards the tops of trees and the line of a long, white sandy beach.

Sandro Elliot said nothing. She dared to glance at him. There was a small furrow between his dark-blond brows. He looked thoughtful.

This has *got* to work—!

The shade of trees encompassed them. Green palmate leaves waved against the cloudless blue sky. The track became an expanse of soft marram grass. The taxi pulled up a few feet before they would have been bogged down in the sand. The driver gestured at the beach ahead, talking rapidly and enthusiastically. Sandro Elliot turned his head and looked coolly at Alix.

Oh shit, what is it? He doesn't look as happy as he did back at the airport.

'Alix . . . why have we come here?'

'It's like the man says – this is hardly ever used, this beach. Even though it's near the tourist hotels. It's because it's difficult to get to. I have a friend who works in the magazine industry: she sorted through their travel files and found me this one – I'm babbling. Sorry.'

The hot meridian sun shone down outside the car, filtering whitely through the trees. Sandro's face was stiff with some emotion – she couldn't tell what.

Abruptly he opened the door, got out of the car, came round to her side and grabbed her elbow as she opened her own door, hauling her out.

'Did you bring insect repellent?' he said harshly. His hand, tight around her biceps, shook her. 'Did you bring water? Food? Sunblock? Cellphone, to call the emergency services when your driver here comes back with his friends to rob the stupid wealthy tourists?'

'What?' Bewildered by the flood of his words, Alix began to shake her head. 'Look, Tommaso's not like that; he's one of the ones my friend interviewed – *no*, I *didn't* bring insect repellent! It's not exactly erotic, is it! Lovemaking on a perfect white beach with the equatorial sun through the palm trees, and "Dear, did you bring the *bug-spray*?"!'

She pulled her arm out of his grip. Stepping back, she stumbled on a clump of the wiry grass. Sand grated against the underside of her foot. She stood on one leg, hooking her finger between her sandal and the sole of her foot to clear it out, and then stood upright again, glaring at the tall blond man.

'What is it you *want*!' she snarled. 'Do you have any idea how much trouble this was to set up? Finding a "tropical beach" I could afford to get us to? Praying for the right weather? Wondering if you'd come here—'

Sweat was running down her body now. The white sun brought painful tears stinging into her eyes. She hadn't brought her sunglasses, she realised; they were sitting on her bed in the hotel – that last, final disappointment was too much. She swore under her breath.

'Palm trees, beach for running naked over the sand – I mean, what else can I *do*?' she yelled.

His expression was utterly cold. He stood by the taxi, oblivious to Tommaso's eager listening face. His eyes were fixed on Alix.

'*You read my fantasy*,' he said. 'You read what I wrote down for Vivienne. You little *bitch*. How did you talk her into that?'

'She doesn't know!'

'That was private!' Abruptly he was red-faced, yelling at her, looking ten years younger. 'That was private: how *dare* you pry into it!'

'I had to! I didn't know what you wanted!'

'I wanted *you*, you dumb bitch!'

Silence.

Nothing but the faint hiss of the white surf on the white sand. And Tommaso's lighter clicking as he lit one of his foul-smelling cigarettes and looked from one of them to the other, his dark eyes brilliant with excitement.

'You going to pay me now and I come back?' he asked. 'Or I get to listen to him yell like a crazy man some more and *then* come back?'

'Oh – shit!' Alix bawled. She stepped towards the taxi and the sole of her sandal slid on the marram grass. She sat down, hard, in the sand. She wiped tears away with the heel of her hand. Looking up at him, she yelled, 'Why did you act like such a shithead, then! I gave you every chance – I fucking threw myself at you! *Why don't you want me?*'

'Yeah,' Tommaso put in, 'why don't you want the lovely lady? I would.'

'Take us back to the airport!' Sandro Elliot unfolded a bunch of notes from his wallet, thrusting them into the driver's hand. He stalked around to the far side of the car and got in, slamming the door. The bang echoed away towards the high volcanic ridges that sheltered this bay from the rest of the island.

'Oh, *fuck* you!' Alix shouted, where she sat, hard enough to make her head swim.

The intense sun beat on her bare arms and shoulders. She explored her shoulder blades with her fingertips. The skin felt tense. *Two minutes and I'm already getting sunburned!*

'*Stupid* bloody fantasy!' she exclaimed.

She stood up, swatting sand off her rump, waved away an insect twice the size of a horsefly and pulled open the taxi door. She slammed down into the upholstery, pulled the door closed behind her, and muttered, 'Get this thing going, Tommaso – I need the air-conditioning!'

'Okay, lovely lady. Say, you want to come for a drink with me, when we drop stupid man back at the airport?'

Alix sniffled and laughed together. She wanted to smile, but her mouth kept going out of shape. 'Thanks, Tommaso – no. I'm getting a plane too. The first one I can get a seat on!'

Laboriously, he turned the car around, smiling regretfully at her in the central mirror. Sandro Elliot gazed out of the far window with stony lack of expression. The drive back up the track to the modern tarmac road passed in complete silence.

Only the cool of the air-conditioning was a welcome sensation. She felt tears trembling at her eyelids and blinked rapidly.

'I've changed my mind,' she said. 'Drop me outside my hotel. As for Mr Elliot – drop him wherever you like!'

The evening sun was gone long before she expected it to be – in the tropics, sunsets are brief. She had a long, cool bath; emerging scented and shaky to lie on her bed, between stages of getting dressed, and look at the stars coming out above the street lights of the town. The noise-level of cars and people singing was just getting into its stride: the evening life would carry on until the early hours here, making up for the fever-hot afternoons spent in siesta.

Alix rubbed vainly at an insect bite and sat up to forage in her bathroom case and dab antihistamine cream on the slight swelling.

That's that, isn't it? A complete bloody waste of time and money . . . Maybe I will go out with Tommaso for that drink. I've got his phone number and he's cute . . .

There was a knock on the door.

Two people knew she was here; for the rest, it could have been room service. Expecting Tommaso, she threw her ivory silk robe on over bra and knickers, and padded across to the door. She opened it. Sandro Elliot stood outside.

'What the fuck do *you* want?' Alix snapped.

'Well, I guess I deserve that,' he said philosophically. He was still wearing the same clothes. The green cotton shirt was sweat-stained now, under the arms and at the base of his strong, corded throat. 'Can I come in?'

'Not unless it's worth me getting undressed for.'

He started. There was a new expression in his eyes that she couldn't quite identify. She stood back, opening the door to the green-and-cream-painted room. After a second, he walked forward and inside.

Does he mean this? Oh, he can't, it's just another mess—

She was instantly hot. She folded her arms firmly over the front of the silk robe, feeling it cling to her hips and thighs as she walked over towards the window shutters. The fact that she had underwear on under her robe made her feel more naked than being naked. Outside the voile curtain tacked over the window, a moth was beating its wings, trying to get to the light.

'What do you want, Sandro?'

'Not what I thought.' His mouth quirked. 'Not *The Blue Lagoon*, and running naked into the surf . . .'

'Yes, I noticed you didn't want that. Or did you just not want it with *me*?' Exasperated, she burst out, 'Do you have any *idea* how much it cost to get tickets at the height of the season?'

Sandro Elliot laughed.

He stood as if ill at ease in the centre of the room, with his back to the mosquito-net-shrouded bed, but his face relaxed as he laughed.

'Fantasies aren't supposed to have a price tag.

Fantasies are free.' He looked at her. 'Alix . . .'

'What?'

'Alix, I have to tell you something.'

She didn't say anything. She clasped her folded arms a little tighter to her body, ignoring the stiffening of her nipples in her bra at his male presence.

'You scare me,' he said simply.

Alix looked at him. He stood with his hands loosely at his side. She could just see, from his chest, that he was breathing a little faster than normal. She didn't look lower to see if he was getting excited.

'I didn't know you were into SM,' she said coolly. 'You didn't write that one down.'

'Not that kinda scared.'

When he reached up to rake back the blond hair flopping over his forehead, she got a waft of stale masculine sweat: the smell of a man who has been out in the heat too long, and who needs to shower. The smell of a real man, not a fantasy. She felt her legs going wobbly. Her high-leg knickers seemed suddenly tight.

No, damn him! I am not letting this man play head games with me any more!

Alix said aloud, 'I'm not letting you play head games with me any more.'

Sandro Elliot nodded. 'Yup. You're right. I have been. And . . . look, it wasn't what I wanted to do. But you should know that the very first time I saw you, you got me so hard – all in a second, you know? And there you were, the ice-maiden—'

'I asked you to fuck me!' Alix protested in outrage. 'That's not exactly "ice-maiden", Sandro, is it!'

'But by then I was scared.'

Something in the honesty of his expression stopped her speaking. For all his outdoor tan, and the sun-lines around his eyes, he looked no older than her now.

'I never had such a strong reaction to any woman,' he said softly. 'I couldn't think about anything else. I dreamed about fucking you – I had wet dreams like a teenager. You were on my mind all the time. And then you started coming out of your shell and doing all those things . . . how could I compare with that?'

His face coloured slightly, and he turned his hands palm outwards, as if presenting himself to her.

'Whatever I did for you, it wasn't going to be good enough. I felt I wanted to make you come harder and longer than any other man or woman ever had. You were obsessing me, but I knew I couldn't satisfy you – so I ran away from you. And from myself.'

His velvet voice saying *make you come harder and longer* sent hot pulses of desire through her groin. She looked up at him, knowing her pupils must be dark and dilated.

'I'm sorry,' he said softly. 'I'd fantasise about you, but I never wrote those down. They were too private. How could I write that I felt like a virgin in front of you?' The skin around his eyes crinkled. 'Because I do. I've never wanted to make love to any woman like I do to you. And then . . .' His voice changed. 'Well, then there'd be what happens in the real world, after a fantasy. And I'm not ready to have my life upset like that. But I still can't get you off my mind.'

'What happens in the real world? Alix wondered.

As if he'd read her thoughts, Sandro added, 'I can't make commitments. I'm going back to the States in the fall.'

'Did anyone ask you to?' Alix said frostily. 'I wanted to fuck you, dear, not live with you. After the boyfriends I've had before I came to college . . . I'm in no hurry to tie myself down like that again. And besides, I'm not giving up Fern.'

'But—' he looked puzzled.

'We've decided to go round Europe this summer.' Alix couldn't help smiling. 'Fern said, and I quote: "We'll give a whole new meaning to sexual tourism!" And then there's at least one other person ... well, never mind. I want who I want, Sandro. This is my sexuality, these are my desires; I don't plan to suppress them because of some—' she took a breath '—some coward who won't come near me until he hears I don't want a wedding ring, and who's frightened of his own hard-on!'

'Okay, I'm not perfect!' he shouted. 'I'm not a fantasy guy with no strings! I worry about whether I can perform, okay? And I worry about clingy women. And I hate for women to ask me out, and I see that you're pissed because I do! I can't help it; I'm a guy; *I* should do the asking! This is just what I am, okay? Sandro Elliot, nothing special, I just want to fuck you till you go unconscious!'

A loud banging on the room wall from somewhere beyond the headboard cut him off in mid-speech. Alix cupped her fingers over her mouth, not sure if she wanted to laugh out loud or swear out loud. She looked up at him: his tired, unshaven face. She was instantly aware of herself, of how he saw her; the silk robe pulled tight across her breasts and hips, the lines of bra-strap and panties, the scent of her, her hair in the lamplight ...

'*Not* unless it's me asking,' she whispered.

His eyes gleamed. He kept his voice down as he said teasingly, 'I'm an insecure guy – what if it makes me go soft?'

'Well, what if it does? You've got fingers and a tongue, haven't you?'

'*Alix!*' His whisper was scandalised, delighted, joyful.

'Don't you "Alix" me! I don't care how puritan the settlers in New England were. You've got to enjoy being filthy if you want to end up in bed with me.'

'What, only the bed? How conventional . . .'

Footsteps went past outside in the corridor: voices shouted up and down the stairs. In the lopsided little whitewashed room, where the floorboards tilted and the bed had one leg wedged up with cardboard, there was tense silence. The moth had abandoned the window. The green paint on the shutters was becoming grey in the starlight; and outside, the prosaic sounds of a town's promenade nightlife went on in the background. The temperature was hot and sticky – but it was either that, Alix had discovered, or live with an airconditioning unit that roared like a jet engine.

'It's no fantasy, is it?' Alix said wryly. 'I've seen cockroaches in the bathroom. We should have taken advantage of your beach, never mind the bugs and the sun-burn. No, wait! *You* wait. I'm going to get this in if it kills me!' She took a breath, and met his gaze. His deep blue eyes were dark and wide with desire. 'Sandro – I'm asking you to fuck me!'

'So you are. I wonder if my masculine pride has gone soft . . .' His deep voice rasped, teasing her, but sounding thick with desire at the same time. His eyes gleamed.

Alix said, 'Why don't I find out. . . ?'

She moved forward, aware at first of being exhausted from the long day spent travelling, and then as she came to stand in front of him, all her weariness vanished. Her flesh tingled at his nearness. She reached up and undid the first button of his shirt.

The material felt warm under her hands, from the warmth of his body. His odour was strong, but pleasing; very masculine – the scent of arousal. She stroked the pad of her forefinger over the tuft of gold-blond hair poking out of his shirt – so soft . . .

Alix moved her hands down, unbuttoning the wrinkled green cotton shirt. His chest came into view, his skin gleaming in the lamplight and his chest hair growing in little knots and whirls. She pressed her hand down into it and slid her fingers up from his belly to the base of his throat. The heat of his skin alone was arousing: she felt her belly flutter and her groin grow hot.

'You know,' he said hoarsely, 'I may not . . . be able to do anything. Don't you tell me that doesn't matter!'

'It doesn't matter as much as you think – but it matters . . .'

She put her hands on his belt, and undid the heavy buckle. The weight of it in her hand was amazing – *only guys wear clothes like this. Sometimes I just love difference.* She didn't allow herself to think of what might be below in his pants. Slowly, she pulled his shirt out of his jeans and peeled it back off his shoulders. With a movement of his muscled arms, he helped her. The shirt slid to the floor.

Alix stepped straight into his embrace.

His arms closed around her. She could feel the strength of them, feel how he tempered it so as not to hurt her. For a second, she felt small. She put her arms around his chest and rested her face against him, smelling the odour of his skin, feeling the softness of his body hair. Fire burned through her veins. She found herself moving her weight on to one leg, so that she could lift the other and rub the inside of her thigh against the outside of his. Pressing herself closer, she licked at his skin, tasting salt. She bent her head down and flicked her tongue across his small, hard nipples.

'Oh, shit, man!' Sandro Elliot groaned.

His arms tightened around her, pressing her to him, all the length of his body. She felt her breasts against his chest, through the bra and silk robe; her thighs pressed against his. And she felt the stiffness of his cock, rising in his jeans.

'Couldn't have put it better myself...' She lifted herself up on to her toes, sliding up his body, and then let herself ease back down. The hanging buckle of his belt caught in the belt of her silk robe. One of his hands left her back and dropped down to wrench it free. Then both his hands were at her shoulders, pushing the robe back, tugging it off her arms – she wriggled and it fell.

She leaned against him, dressed only in bra and panties. She felt the heat of her skin against his skin, sweat slicking their contact, and the heat of her groin against his where his cock tented the front of his pants. Looking up, she lifted herself and put her lips on his.

His mouth was warm and hard under hers. Abruptly, she felt him grip the back of her head, knotting his hand in her hair. He pushed his mouth against hers, sucking at her, and thrust his tongue at her mouth, jabbing between her lips. A searing spark of pleasure went from her throat to her groin, and she moaned under her breath.

'Tell me how you like it...' he breathed into her mouth.

Well, I mostly like not to have to tell...

She broke the contact and looked up at him. One of his hands cupped her buttocks. She felt the warmth through her flimsy panties. His other played with her masses of long hair, not holding her now, but letting her know that he could do.

But it's only in fantasies that demon lovers read your mind.

'I want to undress you. I want you to undress me.'

She gasped air in. 'I want you to fuck me *hard*. Don't worry if I don't come from your cock. I don't always. You can always bring me off with your fingers.'

'Yeah.' His wide, generous mouth spread in a grin. 'Well, maybe you won't have to worry about that. I like to tease . . .'

His hand left her hair. She felt his palm stroking down her back to join his other hand, so that he was cupping both her buttocks. She squirmed against his strong, powerful hands. He dug his fingers in. The sensation made her gasp. She thrust herself forward, grinding against the front of his jeans.

'Now, now . . . we might need that for later . . .'

Sandro put her back at arm's length. Her body felt chilled with the lack of him. She felt her breasts swelling, the straps of her bra tight against her, and her nipples stiffening until they stood out starkly through the soft material. She shifted from foot to foot, rubbing her inner thighs together, as if that could satisfy the aching want in her cunt.

'You've got to fuck me!'

'I thought you wanted to undress . . .' His hands released their grip, trailing around her hips. She felt his fingers stroking the soft flesh of her tummy through her knickers and all but came where she stood. Her knees loosened. She grabbed at his shoulders for support.

'Oh God, take my pants down!' she moaned.

'Not . . . yet . . .' His breathing was harsh and fast. His hand left her stomach, moving up to her right breast, caressing it through the bra. His thumb rasped across the cloth over her nipple. A trail of sparks went through her body, as if there were a wire between her nipple and her clitoris and he had just electrified it.

His other hand clamped down hard over her left

breast. She moaned. It was all she could do to stand up, clinging now to his biceps. She felt her flesh being manipulated by hot, strong fingers, and she ached to have them touching her skin.

'Take it off me!'

He fumbled for a second at the front fastening – not through any ineptitude, she saw. His hands were shaking with how much he wanted her. The front of his jeans had the biggest bulge she'd ever seen.

The bra loosened. She shrugged it away. Taking his hands now, she pressed them to the skin of her breasts. His skin was hot, his palms dry and slightly rough; and as he slid them over her nipples, she groaned and put one hand down to her clitoris.

'Oh, bad girl! Want a spanking?'

'Maybe later,' she gasped. 'Take my knickers off me, I want you inside me!'

He took her wrist, removing her hand from her groin. She felt his other hand pat her buttocks experimentally. She pushed back against him. He landed a hard slap that stung, deliciously, and pushed her up against his body. The hardness of his erect dick through the cloth of his jeans was hot against her belly.

She reached out, grabbed the front of his waistband in her fist and yanked it up. He threw his arms around her shoulders, groaning, his head falling forward on to her shoulder. She felt him squirming in his pants.

'Don't make me come in my jeans!'

'Better get them off, then, hadn't I?'

She let go and popped the buttons of his fly. She had to duck out of his grip to look down and free his cock from the entangling clothes. He wasn't wearing underwear. His thick, red cock jutted out of a bush of gold curls, scrotum swelling, the purple head of his dick glistening with pre-come.

'Always – ready—?'

'Just for you!'

She pushed at his jeans. They slid down his legs. She moved back, for a moment just drinking him in: a half-naked man, with the worn soft denim sliding down in creases around his knees. The sleek line of his body from thigh to hip to chest took her eye, and she feasted on it. Before he could move closer, and without taking her eyes off his torso, she took one side of her knickers between finger and thumb and stripped them down. She all but fell, catching her feet in the cloth as she stepped out of them.

Her nakedness warmed her whole body. She felt her skin hot and tingling. As she watched, he kicked his feet free of his jeans and stood there, stark bollock naked.

'I want to taste you . . .' She sank to her knees on the rough carpet. She clasped her hands to his hips and felt him quiver. Then she dipped her head to his groin, pushing her face into the bush of his hair and sniffing his scrotum. The strong male scent filled her nostrils, and she breathed out hot wet air on him, watching his skin creep and quiver. She extended her tongue and licked at his balls.

'Shiiiit . . . !'

His hands closed, clawlike, on her shoulders. She took his sac into her mouth, wetting it with her saliva, rolling it around with her tongue, and sucking gently as she moved her mouth away from him. She cupped her hand around his glistening balls and very softly squeezed. His cock jerked beside her face. She rubbed her cheek against it, feeling the wetness of his pre-come streaking her skin.

'If you – suck me off—' he gasped, 'that's all you're gonna get. I want to fuck your pretty cunt, lady! I want to stick my big stiff cock right up you!'

'Oh God, *yes*!' she moaned. 'Do it to me!'

His hands were under her armpits, pulling her to her feet. For a second she was pressed against him, naked body to naked body, feeling the velvet of his skin and the rock-hardness of his thick cock. Then he swept her around and almost threw her across the bed. The headboard hit the wall: she didn't notice. She spread her thighs and put her hand between them. Using her fingers, she spread her pink labia, letting him look right up her cunt.

'I got something for you!' he grunted. She had a second to look at him standing, all erect, before he knelt down on the bed and put a hand to each of her knees, spreading her even wider.

His hips dipped forward. He teased her lips with the head of his cock, pressing the hot hardness against her and then drawing back, pressing until his glans almost slipped between her labia, pulling back—

'*Fuck* me!' she whispered intensely. 'Oh God, I want you in me!'

His weight came down on her thigh. She grunted. One of his hands caught her wrists and she let him stretch her arms above her head. The soft bedcover wrinkled under her as she writhed, trying to shove herself on to him. With his other hand, he gripped his stiff, glistening cock. Softly, he brushed it against her thigh, against her buttocks, stroking it over her arsehole and running the head of it around the outside of her labia. Sweat beaded his forehead. His lips were drawn back in a snarl or a grin; she couldn't tell which. She strained against his hands, thrashing her head from side to side.

'Put it in me,' she breathed. 'Put it *up* me.'

'It's – too big for you.'

'I can take anything you've got!'

'Yeah?'

With that, she felt him let go of his cock, resting the tip of it in the entrance to her cunt, and cup his hand around her bottom. Simultaneously, he thrust his cock forward and yanked her arse towards him.

The thick head of his cock slipped in her hot juices, pushed the entrance of her cunt open and stuffed her full. She gasped, hardly hearing it over his groan. Her skin throbbed and shivered. She clenched inside, gripping him, then released as he began to move.

'Ohhh yes . . . ohhhhHHH yes . . .'

She felt his cock move back, and thrust home; move back, and thrust; move back, and thrust; until she was on a border between pain and pleasure, wanting to be filled to the brim, and hardly knowing if she could take his thick throbbing girth. She felt her own juices running down the insides of her thighs. She worked her hips, moving against him, catching his rhythm, feeling his balls banging against her arse.

'Oh, do it – oh, come on and DO IT!'

'Are you the English – ice-maiden?'

'Oh yes!'

'And I'm having you—'

'—yes—'

'—whether you want me to or not—'

'Yes!'

His body hit her, piledriving into her. She kept her rhythm, thrusting her hips, thrusting her hot loosening cunt on to his cock, feeling his balls bang against her, hearing the sounds of sweaty bodies touching and moving, pushing her cunt down on to him, feeling his cock hair rough against her mound, feeling him tilt his body and withdraw a fraction so that his shaft rubbed along the hood of her swollen clitoris—

'Make me come!' she yelled.

'You're gonna! Oh, you're gonna come!'

There was a faint banging on the room wall; she hardly heard it. Nothing existed except hot body against hot body, his thick cock sliding in her cunt, friction frigging her inner walls, and his fingers suddenly moving between them, finding her clit, and brushing the pad of his thumb in a tantalising soft circle—

His mouth dropped to her breast, sucking her flesh in, his tongue flicking and thrusting at her nipple—

His hand, cupping her arse, slid forward, and the tip of his little finger felt her puckering hole and then slid in—

'Oh GOD!' she yelled.

Her arse clamped tight on his finger, her body bucked in an arch off the bed, and she thrust herself up to meet his cock and his finger thrusting down, filling her, filling her full to bursting; and she screamed at the top of her voice as she came, came again, and came for a third time as he jetted inside her, his cum spilling out of her cunt, flowing down her thighs, slicking their bodies as they collapsed together, panting, heaving, exhausted.

'What did you tell him, in the end?' Alix asked.

'That you weren't a whore, you were a beautiful English tourist with the passport to prove it.' Sandro, standing beside her on the promenade and looking out over the Atlantic rollers coming into the town's harbour, smiled. 'I said if he, like, complained to the manager, they'd only think he was jealous.'

'And he bought that?'

'He went away . . .'

'None of his damn' business anyway!'

'He did say the plaster was coming off the wall in his room—!'

Alix snorted. She tried to keep a straight face, but her mouth kept grinning. 'Maybe we *should* do that. We could find a seedy hotel. Pretend you're renting me by the hour.'

'More fun if *you*'re renting a toyboy.'

'Oh?' she said innocently, 'and where would I get one of those?'

They were facing out to sea, so no one saw when he took her hand and placed it over the front of his jeans. She felt his cock swelling, tenting the denim.

He smiled. 'Right there, I guess.'

'You – want to carry on doing this, then?'

He nodded. There was no hesitation there.

'This is the bit you never get to do in fantasies,' he commented. 'If it was a fantasy – well, next time you'd just be my fuck-buddy, and we wouldn't have to go through the bit where you agree to that. Or don't.'

'Or don't,' she echoed. And then, seeing his expression, tightened her hand at his groin. 'Or, I should say: *do*.'

'You sure?'

The wind from the sea whipped her silver-blonde hair into her eyes. It would take a lot of combing later to get out the salt-smelling tangles. But that's the price you pay for standing with your hair streaming in the tropical breeze.

'Risky, isn't it?' Alix said. 'Asking these questions. Waiting for the answers.'

'We can do anything.' He shrugged, loose-boned, grinning down at her with white teeth. The Atlantic wind ruffled his short hair. He still hadn't shaved, and she reached up to touch the irresistible roughness of his chin.

Alix smiled, feeling his warmth beside her. 'A few weeks ago, I thought: there's no substitute for real risk. And you know what? I'm right . . .'

'Anything,' Sandro repeated. 'I know I'm going back to the States and you're going off with Fern Barrie, but we can take time out and meet up. Tell each other what we've been fantasising about while we're apart. What are you smiling about?'

'Oh ... just something I said to Vivienne, once. I must remember to note it down for her – she can put it in her next book.' Alix flattened her hand, feeling the swelling of his cock against her palm. 'That's my fantasy, at the moment – and it's the best fantasy of all. Having someone else to explore all your fantasies with.'

And Alix Neville smiled.